Masquerade
of
Submission

by Carly O'Shea

Masquerade of Submission

Cover Design: Grace Lonsdale

Editor: FionaCampbell

Formatted: Brenda Wright – formatting done wright

Not recommended for readers under 18.

ISBN-13: 978-0692443262
ISBN-10: 0692443266

Table of Contents

Chapter One

Caitlin

Caitlin Leeway escaped to the Northwest Oregon coast whenever life got too overwhelming. Though a mere six-hour drive away, it may well have been a different world, contrasted between the concrete city, where green was only on the perimeter of the sprawling metropolis, and the Oregon coast where the norm was green with the added benefit of the dark blue gray sea, with sporadic clusters of buildings breaking the views.

The freeway, bustling with cars and trucks weaving around her small eco-friendly car, did nothing to help with her stress; the rain that pelted the glass like little knives made it no better. Watching the brake lights on the car in front of her, she tapped the small pedal. Tick. Tick. Tick. Her blinker counted off as the cars in front crawled forward, switching lanes between the cars in front of her, the speedometer that barely registered movement only making her frustration grow.

"Oh yeah, look at that—we finally registered five miles per hour. Lovely. At this rate, I will make it there by, oh, tomorrow. Dammit."

Finally, the large black truck beside her held back, waiting or more than likely distracted by the cell phone or something else; either way, the slight hesitation gave her just the space needed to edge her car into the lane that was actually moving forward. Raising her right hand in a little wave, she gently pressed forward on the gas pedal, grateful to be moving once again. With a quick flick of her hand music streamed from her Bose radio, taking her mind to a different place.

Music was a great equalizer; it drowned out the voices that played in her head: the harping disdain of her mother at her choices, at her existence, really; the other partners at the law firm wanting her to take more cases and do as they say. Everyone wanted *something*... Just not what she wanted, hell, craved. The one that thing she stayed tossing and turning in bed at night thinking about dreamily in years prior, to be that person that could just be taken, wanted, sated; unfortunately, that very desire now woke her up at night with nightmares of un-fulfillment. Was it so bad to want to be desired for who she was? To be cherished? Each day she fought for everyone else. But who was fighting for her? No one, not a single soul; that was all she wanted. Everything was a stressor. Her current stress was the caseload at the law firm and the constant harassment from her mother over her nonexistent love life: the only reason she called now. As though not having one was letting down her family, was a slap in the face to her mother.

When Caitlin reached the midpoint of Olympia, she turned off onto the more peaceful US Highway 101, heading towards the greener forest and beaches of the coast. The lanes went down to two and the cement jungle that had been her view for hours turned into evergreen trees and lush coastal views. It wasn't that she didn't love her apartment, or Seattle for that matter. Caitlin owned the place outright, and after meticulously decorating it, she truly loved it. When she first moved in it was a regular apartment with a great view at the center of everything. Unfortunately, decorating had been limited to pictures hung with removable hooks, and for color she hung sheets of material affixed with fabric adhesive, always keeping a spare can under the cabinet in case a touchup was needed. No painting had been allowed so all the walls were white. She had done what she could to emphasize the view of the Pike Place Market below, the spectacular view of the Puget Sound behind it.

Within a few years she received the letter that the apartments were being converted to private ownership. As each tenant had the right of first refusal, she snapped up her apartment, putting every dime from her savings into the purchase. A few months later her neighbor moved; pulling money from her 401(k) she snapped up that unit as well, and Caitlin went from a comfortable one-bedroom to a three-bedroom apartment with a row of picture windows that spanned the view of the Puget Sound from Vashon Island to Bainbridge Island. Then construction began, followed by weekends spent at Crate and Barrel, while searching every other boutique shop in the market below to decorate it. Each piece was hand selected by her and the result was stunning: elegance and richness combined. Perfect for entertaining and she had done it herself.

She replayed the first time her mother had come to visit. Her mother had turned slowly around the living room, her platinum blonde hair shining in the sunlight streaming in, looking around silently, eyes going over every inch, grading the work. With a shudder, she reached into her hinge-top purse that probably cost more than Caitlin's mortgage payment, pulled out a little card, and broke her daughter's heart. "Call him, he can make this place look presentable."

Turning her car toward the bridge between Oregon and Washington she took a breath; the Columbia River's wide expanse was a sign to her that she was in *her* space. Oregon had been her grandmother's home: escape, the place that held her only happy memories. Here, Caitlin had a small coastal cottage remodeled to her exact specifications, decorated to feel so homey and cozy that there was no doubt when she walked in that it was her sanctuary. Every inch of the place screamed it.

The beach house was her escape. Running away was what she had done for years—what she had seen repeatedly; everyone ran away—from her. Her parents always left her with nannies, or relatives took her in so that they could win the favor of her parents and get money, not because they cared about her. That was never the reason. That didn't change when she started dating. Boyfriends…

Well, that had not been any better for her. Caitlin had a total of three serious men in her past; each had similar qualities: they left her, broke her heart, and eventually her hope.

The beach, on the other hand, did not hurt her. The water lapped at the sand, gentle or rough, and always came back at the turn of the tide, unlike every other person in her life. Caitlin started protecting herself, seeing the signs: the pulling away, working late, or worse—mysterious phone calls where she could just hear the female voice on the other end of the line, quickly taken to other rooms. Caitlin would cut ties, usually in a note, email, or the like; rather than having her heart destroyed, she would close it off and leave. Avoiding emotional confrontation was her first inclination. Honestly, Caitlin did not think her heart could take any more heartbreak.

She needed the peace, the stability that the coast provided. The gray, overcast skies were familiar, easy, and matched her mood. Caitlin was a brilliant attorney, yet there was nothing in her personal life—complete emptiness. Michael, her ex, said exactly that before slamming the door on both her and their relationship. She was a hollow shell— heartless. Turning up the volume on her radio, she tried her best to stop the tears of frustration at her waste of a life that seemed to be swallowing her up, concentrating on the drive as sad songs released the tears, cleansing her if only for a moment. A few hours later Caitlin was pulling into her drive, the small cottage coming into view. Parking her car, Caitlin grabbed her bag out of the back seat and headed up the steps toward the birch door.

***

A few hours later she was completely cozy in a pair of heather gray yoga pants and a long soft tank top worn from years of use, sipping on freshly brewed coffee. Setting down the steaming cup, she looked out of the big picture window that had cost her way too much money and frustration during the remodeling process. During one of her many trips to the coast, she found the 1940s fishing cottage while stopping at garage sales. The *For Sale* sign's paper was deteriorated to a dull pink from the salty sea air. After walking through the tiny space, she found that she could just see the home as she would have it and placed an offer immediately. Three months and a wiped savings account later, she was the proud owner of a two-bedroom Rockaway beach home, with a direct ocean view and a private trail through the dunes in the small, quaint town of Depoe Bay.

A smile crossed her face at the sound of crunching gravel and a little red sports car came into view through the picture windows, winding around her house to the carport— dust from the gravel drive a cloud behind the wheels. Waving, she headed out the French doors onto her deck to meet Sarah, her best friend. Sarah had called earlier that day declaring that she just had to see her immediately, and had already started the long drive down from Seattle for the weekend. Why the urgency, she had no clue, but knowing Sarah, it was going to be an interesting story. She needed the distraction.

"Well hello, stranger," she called out as she made her way down the steps, greeting Sarah with a hug at the bottom.

"I'm not the stranger here. You, little missy, are."

Sarah was a free spirit. They had been friends since college; after a few years in law school, Sarah had changed her mind and declared that law was out and therapy was in. Since that day, she had been Caitlin's self-proclaimed personal therapist. The two were the picture of complete contrast: Caitlin the clean cut, straight-laced family attorney

12

with long auburn hair, perfectly trimmed; Sarah the flower-child-transplant from a previous era, whose hair color and length changed by the week and sometimes the hour.

She felt her friend's arms squeeze her just a bit too tightly before releasing her. Each taking a bag from the pile on the ground, they headed inside and out of the misty sea air.

"Okay, so what is going on? It sounded important and well... I was worried a bit that you wouldn't tell me." Caitlin sat on the soft, queen-sized overstuffed bed in the second bedroom, watching as Sarah unpacked her bags. The stark difference between the bright bohemian colors of Sarah's bags and the soft pastel blue and white the room was decorated with made her smile. The room's sea motif made it as though you walked into a lighthouse. Small round port windows lined one wall at eye-level height, giving you that at-sea feel. It had been one of her favorite rooms to do, and it made her immensely happy to share with her friends who came to visit.

"Well, you bolted. Again."

Caitlin caught the eye roll and thick sarcasm in her tone of voice, and quickly interjected. "I did not bolt. I just

13

wanted—no, needed—a break. Big difference, Sarah."

"Really? Couldn't tell. Oh, and the fact no one other than your secretary knew you were leaving really does mean bolt. Maybe we need to get you a new dictionary. One with personal examples, or better yet: pictures, a stunning play-by-play, HD video, or something. You know, for a smart attorney, I would say that you are really not that perceptive when it comes to little ole you."

Caitlin shook her head and followed Sarah to the kitchen, settling into the breakfast nook and picking up an apple from the bowl in the middle of the table filled just moments ago with groceries brought from the city market, and watched as her best friend took over the large wood surface with her laptop and assorted multi-colored notebooks.

"How long are you staying? Not that I really care, you can stay for as long as you want, but um, just curious. I did see the load of bags you brought." She smirked at her friend, who stuck her tongue out in answer.

"Hey, this is light! And this is all here for a purpose, thank you, miss grumpy."

She took a big bite out of her apple, crunching overtaking the room, as Sarah, mesmerized by whatever was on her computer screen, thwacked loudly on the keys.

"What purpose is that? I'm really rather afraid to know, but what the hell, lay it on me."

Caitlin was about to take another bite into the juicy apple when she caught her friend's serious look.

"You are. I get that your parents are terrible and that your love life has been…shall we say less than stellar, but now…it is time. I—you can thank me later—have decided that you must start moving on with your life. I know you're a bit shy, sooooo, I thought this was perfect."

When Sarah turned the laptop around and the Masquerade website came into view, her first reaction was to reach out and shut the lid. But the realization that her friend was trying to be nice won out. Instead, she shook her head.

"No, and by that I mean…thank you, but no thank you." Taking another bite of the apple, she started fiddling with the papers on the table, acting as if there were something very interesting in the local paper—which there wasn't really, but she was *not* going to let on about that.

"Why? You have to give me a good reason, not just some stupid one. Come on, try. Give me a good one; I figured you would, so I've been practicing all my answers."

Tilting her head, Caitlin grinned. Sarah knew her well and she had just done the right thing, there was no way she was going to just let that go. She had to one up her on reasons… Years of doing just that egged her on.

"Well, let's see. Online dating…." Her eyes rolled, a look of annoyance clear on her face. "My opinion. Really, the pictures are old, I'm talking from high school, or oh yeah better yet, he's locked up in prison; do you really want me to continue?" Caitlin gave Sarah a serious look, wagging her finger as she shook her head. "I'm not interested. I have a career, one that requires me to have a good reputation and a perfectly spotless background. Hello, I'm in family law! I watch marriages fail regularly. I write pre-nuptial agreements, because marriages… do… not… work. Moreover, this is what over half of my clients come in saying: 'I met them online. They were one person online… After the wedding, they became someone very different.' I have seen it time and time again. I just can't."

"No!" Sarah said emphatically, causing Caitlin's eyebrows to raise. Sarah stood, pointing and gesturing as if her life depended on it. Her friend was always so passionate; it was one of her favorite qualities about the woman. Right now though, it was not funny or cute. Caitlin hated making her feel bad. After all, Sarah was well intentioned. Unfortunately, Caitlin just couldn't see a relationship in her future.

"You have to give this a chance. Look, a masquerade-style date. No faces, no names, no nothing. It's completely perfect. Planned by the service, so before you say anything, all you have to do is get dressed. They even handle the transportation. And… it's naughty. I mean, take those books we read on the beach, the ones that we say could never be real. Well, this site caters to it. Please? You have to say yes. I paid for your membership, so there." Sarah stuck out her tongue. "You, Miss I-can't-I-won't-I-don't-want-to, are going to try online dating. If you do not set up your profile before I leave on Sunday, well then I will, and so help me God, you will not like how I do it. So if you're as smart as I know you are, you will get your profile set up yourself."

"I'll think about it, okay? But I am definitely not promising anything." Caitlin could tell there was not going to be instant agreement, so it was better to just let it drop.

"Fine. Think about it while I run to the store. I want to get a movie from the machine."

Caitlin, wondering how to handle this mess, watched as Sarah headed out the door. She had no idea how to convince her friend not to push for a relationship for her; she had accepted she was wounded property, damaged goods. No, there was no magical answer to her problems, no solution for the lack of a relationship, no fixing her. Air— she needed it and she needed it *now*. She darted to her room, her feet hitting the wood floor the only sound as she passed through the open living room to the wide hallway. Slipping out of the worn yoga pants and tank top, she threw on a pair of khaki shorts and a white tank top, grasped the oversized hoodie that hung by the back door, and strode out to the beach.

The ocean breeze whipped her long auburn curls. It was really an act of God to keep them from turning into a knotted mess, and today was no different. With a hairband on one wrist and her fingers tangled in the mass of hair, she did her best to contain the strands twisted by the wind. Giving up, she pulled the hoodie up above her head and started down the path she had been traveling back and forth on for years now. There was a natural path through the tall brush and dunes, the sand between the grassy mounds usually clear, warmed by the overcast sky. Paying absolutely no attention to the path, she inhaled sharply as one minute she was walking, the next falling when her feet encountered some unseen object.

"Here, let me help you." The raspy male voice startled her; it was one of romance novels and good, sultry music—the kind that, despite any control a woman had, would make her clench her thighs at the sound's vibration. And she was no different. Pushing her head the rest of the way through the sweatshirt, her hair now out of her vision, her eyes swept across the hard lines of a drop-dead gorgeous man, who in every way fit his sexy voice. His chest was chiseled from what had to be hours of exercise— no way someone was that muscular naturally—and his face pure Adonis.

Realizing she was staring and it was getting a bit uncomfortable, she smiled. "No, it was my fault, really," she stammered. "I should have been watching where I was going."

His lighthearted laugh made her pause. "Well, try to avoid the driftwood next time. Can't have a pretty little thing like you getting hurt out here."

She watched as he smiled before jogging off down the path. "Great, the first guy I ever see here not old enough to be my grandfather, and I make a fool of myself." Standing, she brushed the sand off herself and continued down the beach toward the lighthouse.

As she walked along the waterline, her mind wandered back to the stranger with the sexy voice. His eyes were a deep blue that she imagined, in the right light, would look like steel. Giggling, she realized his eye color described him completely: his body looked all hard and muscular, he was perfect, and definitely not something she had seen on this beach before. Hell, she would sure never get upset with him for leaving crumbs in bed! Glancing up at the seagulls drifting on the wind streams, she did everything to stop thinking about the sexy stranger. "Not what I need right now. He probably has a girlfriend or wife. Anyone that sexy must. Plus, I do not need a relationship. I need to be strong and independent."

She walked until she could see the cliffs that led up to the lighthouse clearly. Knowing she was in no way ready for a trek of that magnitude, she turned around and followed her footsteps back toward her beach house. Sarah was going to be back soon, if she wasn't already, and that dating site discussion was not going to go away. If Caitlin wanted to have anything to say about what was in or out of her profile, she had better get going on it. If not, Sarah would no doubt make and post the profile herself and there was no telling what she would put in it. Shaking her head, Caitlin toyed with the idea of starting it and just leaving it. Maybe that would be enough to shut Sarah up. Her friend never said she actually had to date, just set up the profile. Laughing, she headed back, feeling a bit better about the situation.

Approaching the house, she stomped on each step in an effort to knock off as much sand as she could from her feet. Peeling off her sweatshirt, she threw it on the hook that hung by the door leading to the kitchen, before sitting down in front of her laptop at the built-in desk in the kitchen. Pushing the little glowing power key, the screen flashed to life, its gentle light a comforting friend. Clicking the widget for email, she watched the latest batch fill her inbox.

"That better be my best friend working on that profile. Tick tock. Tick tock." Caitlin turned to see Sarah flopping down on the couch, remote in one hand and an aluminum pouch in the other.

She hit the tab key on the screen and opened the link that Sarah had sent her earlier. "I am, as a matter of fact, starting the profile now." She gave her friend a smug see-if-you-can-threaten-me-now look and turned back to the laptop. Waiting for the website to load, she looked to the refrigerator, thinking of the drink her friend was enjoying. "Did you buy any more of those adult juice boxes?"

"Hell yes, I stocked you all up. An assortment of fruit flavors, mojitos, daiquiris, and long island iced teas galore! Definitely grab one, it will make the profile better; loosen you up a bit."

"Thanks, don't mind if I do." Pulling out the drawer-style freezer, which she really loved, she grasped one of the mojito-flavored pouches. Pulling the built-in straw from the back, she unsheathed the plastic tube before taking the pointy end and firmly stabbing it in the round circle at the top. Making short order of the hardness by squishing the pouch in her two hands, Caitlin took a quick pull on the straw. The icy cold drink hit her tongue and she had to squeeze her eyes shut as she gave herself a brain freeze.

"You're stalling. Get to the profile. I have a movie to watch and you're interrupting me."

Gently laughing as she shrugged her shoulders, Caitlin started filling out the online dating questionnaire. She flew through the first part, filling out all the basics. Fingers mindlessly played with the auburn ringlet that had fallen over her shoulder as she typed. When the questions went from basic to more personal, she laughed and caught herself looking over her shoulder before she answered. It almost felt as if Sarah could see her deepest, darkest desires; not that she didn't already know them. Hell, they told each other pretty much everything. Sarah had done all the things Caitlin had dreamed of, and when she came home from her dates, her friend would regale her with the stories.

Still, the fear that Sarah would find out that she was some sex-fiend hit her cold in the stomach, churning the mojito that now resided there. She had a higher than normal sex drive; her ex-boyfriends had said she was deviant. Hell, she had all but worn out her past lovers, not that there had been that many. "Desired amount of sex per day?" With a sigh, she looked at her options: daily, twice daily. Her mouse hovered over the twice daily. With a quick laugh, she clicked the circle and hit send. *Hmmm, can't hurt*, she thought as she pushed away from her desk to head to the shower to clean up before bed. "I'm going to go take a shower."

"You did hit send, right? Because you know I'll just log in and do it for you if not," Sarah quipped.

"It's sent. So now we get to see just how pathetic I really am. My money is on no responses. Showering now. Enjoy your movie. Love ya."

"Love you too, crazy girl." Sarah's voice was softer, and she heard the TV's volume go up a notch.

At five foot-seven, Caitlin was taller than most girls, not fat, just not skinny either, at 150 pounds she was pleasantly in the middle. Cushy was the description her granny had used. She was happy with her curves—in a little black dress, heads always turned. Turning the dial on the shower, she tapped her long red painted fingernails on the ceramic tiles that lined the wall before stepping into the

24

steaming water.

Warm water fell on her skin, washing away all the tension and stress. Her mind drifted to the man she had seen on the beach—his eyes, that voice. A moan escaped her lips as she thought of him. Her hand slid over her breasts, nipples responding to her knowing touch and becoming hard nubs. Continuing lower, she imagined it was the stranger's hand sliding down her stomach lightly, over her pelvic bone to the breach of her sex. Deft fingers, knowing exactly what would feel good, slipped between already moist folds, finding the hardened nub.

Caitlin's teeth grazed her bottom lip as her ministrations continued with just the right pressure, teasing and toying until desire pulsated deep inside her core. Pinching her nipple with one hand, two other fingers slid deep inside, bringing her climax close. Thrusting in and out, she matched each thrust with the pinch of a nipple, giving just the right amount of pain needed to find release. The climax shuddered through her body as she let out a deep breath. It was just a stopgap—she needed a man.

The feel of a strong male body next to hers, touching, caressing in that not-so-gentle fashion always sent her spiraling over the edge of true passion. An edge she couldn't find while pleasuring herself. With a sigh, she rinsed all signs of self-pleasure off, stepped out of the shower, and dried off. Looking one last time out the window, waves shone in the light of the full moon in a rare, cloudless sky. She slid into her king-sized bed and tossed fitfully as the stranger dominated her thoughts until she fell asleep.

Chapter Two

Gavin

"Is this all that was submitted?" With an almost-growl, he questioned his assistant over the phone. Looking at the laptop screen, he could see all the files submitted or at least passed on to him. "Not acceptable, this is an established client; contact him, Shelly. I cannot take a week off to 'relax', as you like to call it, if, on the first day, this is what happens. I am counting on you." Hearing her rambling apologies and assurances that she would be on top of everything, he thanked her and hung up.

As a successful marketing manager, Gavin McDonald knew what it took to get noticed. He had built his business from the ground up from an office out of his home with him as the sole employee to a large advertising and marketing agency in the Pike Place Market District of Downtown Seattle. In the 15 years building his company he had taken two vacations: both relatively short. But after years of prodding from his assistant Shelly, who had been with him since he had finally hired staff, he was taking a real vacation—well, as real as it could get in the hand-me-down agate beach house he received from his parents when they passed.

Hell, he could take anything, work a bit of advertising magic, and next week everyone would want it. Even those who didn't would buy it just so they weren't left out. God forbid the world didn't keep up with the Joneses. It was that warped thought that really kept him in demand by every major company in the Pacific Northwest. He understood people. Yet, ironically, he was alone.

He had doubts of finding the *right one,* as everyone said. He had needs... desires. And the regular girl next door... usually not interested. His idea of a great date was just like every other guy's, except for the fact that he liked his nights to end in a hot sex scene he controlled. That was *not* the norm. Smirking, he kicked his feet up on the desk that sat directly across from a spectacular view of the ocean. He watched seagulls diving into the water, weaving between each other in a well-choreographed dance. Out of the corner of his eye, he saw an elderly couple walking by hand in hand. They looked happy—in love.

"They probably don't do half the things I want, which is why they work. They give and take. One is not completely in control," he spoke aloud to the beta fish swimming serenely in the bowl on his desk, its complete existence reliant on him. His friends had laughed at the time he spent catering to the fish's needs, from testing the water with the little stick that evaluated the chemical levels, to making sure the proper nutrients were leveled out by finding just the right plant to float on the surface of his crystal bowl.

His mind drifted to the girl he'd seen earlier during his run. She was something, his body reacting at the thought of her. He had wanted to wrap his fingers up in her mass of curls and claim her pouty mouth. He had no idea why, really. She seemed clumsy, and apparently not very observant since she had tripped over the driftwood log very plainly lying in her path. Something in her emerald green eyes, her lush red lips, all surrounded by a halo of red hair sent his desire surging into overdrive. It took everything he had to jog away. The only thought strong enough to propel him down the beach was that he did not want to go through the mess that always followed his attempts at finding *the one*. He had a rule: no novice women; only those who knew and understood what he offered, what he was willing to give, and what he demanded in return. Reminding himself of that alone was enough. The stranger on the beach would be too much temptation. One second's look in her eyes and he was imagining her on her knees, her plump lips surrounding his cock.

Diverting his stare to the other side of the room, his eyes came to rest on the blinking light of his archaic answering machine. He had meant to throw it out ages ago, but it wasn't broken and well, if it's not broken, why fix it? So it stayed and he forgot to check it for days, sometimes weeks. Making his way across the room, he hit the flashing button and heard the machine kick into gear, rewinding the tape inside that was probably ready to disintegrate. The high-pitched whine of his ex-girlfriend came out of the speaker, rattling off a message about how she missed him and would he please call her. Shaking his head, he frowned when he heard the almost year-old date at the end. "That figures. Never did get that message."

Natasha moved out over a year ago, and made it perfectly clear why.

"I get you want me to be submissive in the bedroom. I get you want to be in complete control. I have done that, haven't I?"

He looked up at her as she stood in front of the heavy double doors to his Seattle penthouse. "Yes, you have done just that." He glanced at the bags at her feet; neatly stacked and bursting full with everything he had ever bought her.

"Well then, I am serious, Gavin, you need to make a choice. Look at me. Look at these bags. I am serious this time. I will leave, walk out the door, and never, ever come back. I want a ring. A shiny ring on my finger, one that says you are claiming me. Hell, I don't even have a collar, and all the girls at the club that are in an exclusive relationship with their Dom... they have that. I don't. I look like a fool. Don't I mean something to you? I mean really?"

He turned away from her, not giving her the respect of an eye-to-eye conversation. "Sorry, you don't mean to me what you want to. You are a good submissive. Not great. Good. I don't feel the way you are looking for and I never

31

will. I suggest we just let this go with that. Thank you; it's been fun."

The shriek of her indignation forced him to turn toward her. "Listen here! I have been great to you, letting you do whatever you want to me. I never complained. I did everything. I played the perfect hostess for you at the club. What more do you want? Why do you think I was only 'good'? What else can I do?"

He calmly looked into her eyes. "The fact that you just asked for a ring and a collar... Well honey, that right there is why you and I will never be. You presume way too damn much. Secondly, I don't have a life just at the club. Ever wonder why you were never involved in it? You don't fit there. I never saw you there. I didn't want to be so cold, but you're just not getting it." He picked up the cell phone lying on the table beside him and pushed the button that direct dialed the front desk. "Please send someone up. My guest is leaving now." He turned back to her and smiled. "See you around." He ignored her huffing and puffing as well as the sound of the doorman coming in from the lobby of the 20-level building to get the bags.

"Please put her in my car, have my driver take her

wherever she asks."

The doorman just nodded. "Yes, sir."

Hearing the alert on his computer letting him know he had another email, he came out of his memories and clicked the icon. With his unique desires and proclivities, the need for special methods of finding dates was paramount. He was not into just going to local clubs. Hell, that was where he met every one of his past submissives, and none to date truly called to him. Even the more discriminating private clubs seemed filled with tourists. He had played it for years, and was just not interested in that scene anymore. He had everything he needed in the privacy of his home and now in his escape. The clubs were just not what he was looking for; the pressure to be the cookie cutter expectation of a Dom was not what he wanted. He knew he was different; yes, he wanted to have someone submit to him. He had no doubts about that. However, he also wanted it to be something unique, just what they needed in their relationship. The only thing missing from his perfect life— her, the one who literally filled the space in his heart, his soul, his very life that right now sat so empty and dormant. Scanning the email, his pulse quickened.

Gavin,

Hope you are well. Attached is a match that I thought would be of interest to you. You know the routine, darling, click the button and I will set the wheels in motion.

As always,

Yours.

The information sheet gave the list of preferences and hard limits. "Hmmm, good match." Clicking the button, he reached down and adjusted his already responding cock. Within twenty-four hours, he would have a date set—all parts of the first meeting always completely arranged by the agency—the contract delineating his specifications for submissive relationships drawn up and at the location in a sealed envelope waiting for them.

He was looking forward to this. His best friend Matt had given him the agency information after using them. He smiled as he thought of Matt and Sonja; their wedding the previous weekend had been a happy occasion, filled with joy and passion that was so obvious to everyone there. Matt and Sonja were more than in love. It had given him hope that maybe, just maybe, there was a chance someone out there could fill his needs and he could fulfill theirs. How many people out there had a lavish wedding and a collaring ceremony all in one day? True, only a few had been witness to the latter portion of the day, but that to him had been the more meaningful. He had seen marriages come and go. They were pieces of paper with delicate embossing, yes, but just paper. His life was proof that the paper was meaningless. After watching his mother go through four different marriages before he was even out of high school, he had realized it was no true commitment. Collaring was a commitment of lifelong proportions, not something taken lightly.

Getting up from his desk, he headed into the lavish bedroom and attached bathroom that he had custom built to his exact specifications. The stone floor was heated to just the right temperature, so that one never needed to wake and walk across cold floors; perfectly matched cabinets; large walk-in shower; separate soaking tub—it was a work of art more than anything and definitely not something you expected to see in a small, oceanfront cottage. Pulling his shirt off, he tossed it into the hamper, joined quickly by his jeans. Hitting the button for setting Number 1 on the digital screen, water came on to just the right temperature through multiple jets. Stepping into the stone enclosure, he was glad he had invested in the instant heat options. The warm water cascading over him relaxed him, letting his thoughts wander. His hand gripped his swollen member, sliding up and down the shaft with just the right amount of twist. He pictured mystery beach girl's pouty lips wrapped around his cock. The feel of his cock enveloped in the moist heat of her mouth created a rhythm that quickly relieved the pressure in his sack. Finishing his shower, he stepped out, dried off, and strode to look out the French doors at the moon shining on the water. The sound of the rough surf created the perfect lullaby; he yawned and slipped into bed.

Chapter Three

The Agency

The glass door to her office swung wide. Annabelle turned to see who was disturbing her relative peace. "Good morning, Tish, whatever has you running around like a crazy person this morning? Anything good, or just another sale on the energy drink of the month again?"

Annabelle Deveroux smiled as she playfully picked on her assistant of four years at the Masquerade. Tish Holloway had been her assistant for as long as Annabelle had been in the matchmaking business. Before that, the woman had been the waitress who served her coffee every morning at the diner down the street from her office in the Queen Anne area of Seattle. Annabelle had seen something in her then—the drive to succeed and compassion, which she rarely saw in most people. Tish had kept her daughter in a booth in the corner, letting the child color on different sheets of paper while she handled as many customers as possible. Then, miraculously, some other waitress would get up from her lazy ass where she had been hiding in the back, and come out and help, more than likely coming out just in time to pick up the tip that was just laid down. Tish cared. Every morning the waitress would ask if she had a good night. When business picked up enough, Annabelle made her an offer to come work for her, even arranging for daycare in the building where they worked. Company paid, of course. The one thing Annabelle could not handle was seeing a good person given the shitty end of the stick.

"Annabelle, you know every morning is fun with you." Tish set down the coffee she had been carrying and with a small huff sat herself on the corner of the couch on the far side of the large room. "And, no, I have not had excessive amounts of energy drinks. It's just a happy day; the sun is shining and you know how rare that is." Tish looked around the room; that meant one thing to Annabelle: something was coming, some discussion she didn't want to have, more than likely the same one as always. "You've been busy today. Always helping others. I just don't understand why you don't have others help you with the matching."

Annabelle looked over and gave her a little grin. "We have always run this company this way. We always will. Plus, I have plenty of time."

Tish rolled her eyes. "Of course you have plenty of time. You have plenty of time because you do not date. Imagine that: the matchmaker who doesn't date." She stood up and placed the files she had brought with her on the desk.

"These are your newest files, all organized and ready for you. Best of luck on your matching but me... I'm off to the corner store. Locking the door on my way out, see ya in a bit."

Annabelle watched her walk out of the room, shaking her head and smirking at the young woman. *Youth.* "Have fun!" Annabelle called out as she turned back to the computer, saved her document, and looked at the delivery. Picking up the files, she quickly glanced over each one, analyzing each and every line for anything that would fit one of her current clients. *Well, I'll be.* The file in her hand was perfect for the file she had been just looking at. She could tell the clients' answers were just different enough to be interesting, yet enough alike to have years of companionship. Continuing through the file, she rifled through her desk and found the other file. Putting them side-by-side she smiled; yes, these two would be perfect. She was longing for something, and he was trying to find someone to give that same something to—Perfect Match.

Her fingers clicked furiously, the sound like little pings from a machine gun as she typed the emails out for the two clients. One had been a personal recommendation from a previous client, a special case. She had already met the gentleman. Business by day, Dom by night. This would be a great match. She just knew it.

Annabelle finished the letters for other matches and looked at her to-do list sitting beside her on the desk. Old-fashioned to some, her worn leather date book—once a vibrant red, now a dull burgundy from years of use—was filled with lists and multicolored lines. Each one meant something to her, and only a select few understood it. Picking up the phone, there were many arrangements to make in a short amount of time. Drivers, dinners, and, of course, the signature masks for the dates. Each one given out was original, handmade, and unique to the person she had them made for.

"Hi, it's Annabelle. I need two more masks."

"Two more?" Leonard questioned, his voice shaky yet commanding. He had been her supplier for the masques since she came upon his work at a shop in Kirkland; the older man was not just a vendor to her, he was an artist.

"Yes. Same setup as before. I will email the description of the clients over now. I do not want to be that involved. I trust your style and design."

"Annabelle, when do I make one for you? No charge. You do so much for everyone else. When is it your turn?"

"None for me. No time. You know how it is; running a business is a full-time, life-consuming notion. But thank you; I will send the driver over to pick them up tomorrow." With the last of the arrangements made, she slid the chair back and smiled before she realized that she was once again alone. Picking up the remote to the television in the corner, she pushed the little red button and tried to catch up on the daily news.

Chapter Four

Caitlin

Having spent the morning doing absolutely nothing and feeling rather decadent because of it, Caitlin sat in front of her laptop, mouth hanging open, eyes wide with amazement. She knew that there was a chance they would find someone, albeit remote, but a chance nonetheless. A date set in less than twenty-four hours—not what she expected.

Her hand grazed over the keys of the laptop, trepidation filling her, eating at her. She had been so sure that it would be a while before they matched her or even found someone remotely close that she had never even contemplated the next step. What was she thinking? How was she going to go through with this when she couldn't even talk about it? This guy sounded like he really knew the lifestyle. Hell, she was starting to think, as she read his profile through for at least the fifth time, that he might be completely fake, some made-up person taken from the last erotica novel she had read. The one that had telltale signs of years of repetitive reading. The worn pages now relegated to a drawer beside her bed, the go-to book for a lonely night.

"Do it."

Caitlin turned her head around and found Sarah peering over her shoulder. The benefit of the floorplan was everything really opened up into this main area. The heart of her home was this room; it served as the kitchen and the family room. And right now, well, she was grateful for the distraction Sarah was able to provide because of that design choice.

"Easy for you to say." She turned back toward the screen, the sound of dishes and pots and pans being moved around in the kitchen behind her a ready diversion. The sounds of the ocean could be heard over the occasional chop of a blade or as one of the dishes clanged. She silently thanked her friend for coming in; food sounded good and the smells that wafted over to her made her stomach growl.

"It is easy. It's the easy way to solve the problem

43

we have been facing. Yes, *we,* before you interrupt. Do you think I find it easy to watch you go through life in a shell? You deserve love, and you could have it, but you don't let yourself. Every time you get close, or someone gets close to you, you dart away like a wounded rabbit. It hurts to watch you, it really does. Please, just do it. Try one time for me, and if this doesn't work, then I'll never push again. Hell, I'll be your 'plus one' forever if it doesn't."

The heartfelt words struck Caitlin. Sarah cared for her—*cared*. This singular fact meant she should at least try. Hell, one bad date and her friend would be her "plus one" forever. Sounded like a deal. Besides, maybe this would give her a chance to figure out how to make it not quite so miserable for Sarah to be her friend.

Quickly, she replied that she would attend the masquerade before she could get nervous and chicken out. Once the response left her outbox, she was stuck. She never liked to break a commitment—she'd trapped herself. Laying her head on the desk in front of her, she closed her eyes in frustration, fear, and a multitude of other emotions.

"No, no, no. Why, why, why?" Sitting up, she scooted back from the table, her eyes drawn to the sand just

44

outside the door. "God, I need a walk." Standing, she slipped her feet into her tennis shoes, grabbed her iPod and earbuds, slipped them in the pocket of her yoga pants, and headed toward the back door to the beach.

"I'll be right back," she called as she headed out.

"Okay, quiche will be ready in an hour and a half. Don't be late, or I'll eat the whole damn thing."

She could see clouds on the horizon, tried to gauge the speed in which they were moving. They were definitely rain clouds, but looked to be moving slow enough for her to get to the lighthouse and back. She made her way in good time, her mind completely bombarded with fears and insecurities as she walked. *What if I only think I want the dominant man? In real life, he could be very different, not at all what I want. What if a man like that doesn't want me; I mean, why would he?*

When she reached the jetty jutting out below the lighthouse on the cliff, she stopped and evaluated the lapping waves, watching them surge ahead before pulling back. The tide was heading in, and the beach still held a large expanse of sand. The jetty was easily reachable. She headed out, completely ignoring the imposing clouds that

45

were quickly coming closer.

Systematically, she maneuvered through the big chunks of cement and rock, being careful to not slide and end up breaking an ankle or, worse yet, falling in the water, where the thrashing waves would pound her into the rocks and take her life in the process. Climbing the rocks, she found the perfect perch: the rock with a perfectly flat top, one she had used many times before. Her vantage point allowed her to see the tide pools—the colorful life in each creating a peaceful vision almost like an abstract painting. Beautiful, at least to her. Her earbuds securely placed in her ears, she was relaxed in her own little world. A tap on her shoulder came as a start, causing her to almost slip.

"Hey, sorry, didn't mean to scare you." His large hand clasped onto her arm to keep her from falling.

"Oh, hello." Caitlin once again found herself looking into familiar steel blue eyes. "We keep running into each other." Smiling, she tried to keep her heart from racing. "I didn't see you; sorry that I jumped. I'm Caitlin." She watched his face shift to a sexy smile. *Dammit, does everything he does come off so damn sexy?*

"Gavin McDonald, and it's nice to officially meet

you. I just stopped to tell you that you may want to get moving, it looks like a storm is coming on pretty quick."

"Thanks!" Looking at the sky, she smiled as she stepped over the boulders in an effort to head to the sand before the rain soaked them, making them more slippery than they already were. She could feel and hear him following her toward the sandy beach. Turning as she stepped off the jetty, she held out her hand. "Thank you again. I truly appreciate it. I know those rocks can get slippery." Pulling out her cell phone, she clicked the little button on the top. As the time illuminated the screen, she realized that the quiche was probably out of the oven and in the process of being savored, but not by her. "Wow, it's getting pretty late. I better get going." With a quick smile, she turned and started walking. *Please, oh please, don't follow me.* She had only hours left until she would meet her mystery man, the contractually perfect man, and now of all the possible times during this messed-up life of hers, fate was presenting her with a spectacularly handsome man. A handsome specimen of male flesh so naturally sexy, she could feel her thighs clenching just thinking about him.

"You know, this is the second time we have met on

this beach." She turned at the sound of his voice—raspy, deep, and definitely sexy.

"Yes, this is true. Apparently we frequent the same places for our workouts," she said with a laugh as she noticed his workout wear. As they walked, they talked about the local weather and the different things they saw, but she made sure to keep the whole conversation light. She listened to him tell her all the details of the recent house he had come into possession of. "Well, if you ever need any good contractor information, I'd be happy to give you some names. I had a really good group to help with mine."

"Thanks, I appreciate that. I never really came out here much. So it's all a bit new to me. Different world I guess." His voice was a drug easing through her mind, wiping the thought of anything away.

Concentrate, Caitlin thought. *Concentrate…. I have a date tonight… Not the time…* "Very much so. It's a bit slower and really, we may be the only people that are not here in the prime of our retirement." *Ok, I got this… Look at me go… I have complete control. Sexy, hot man or not. I have this on lock.*

His laugh. That was all it took.

48

Her mind was focused, had to be; if not, she knew she would not be able to help but picture that toned chest above her as she lay tied to the table, his hands running along her body, and God knew that she didn't need to think that. Hell, this was a complete stranger and she lacked a filter in some ways. Ok... Most ways. And right now... She was tied to the table... in her mind...

"Are you okay?" She was brought back to the here and now, hoping he couldn't tell she had been lost in a moment of complete sexual desire thinking of him.

"Yes, sorry, a bit distracted. Well...this is my house. Thank you for, you know, saving me from the rain." She stood smiling, mesmerized by him. When his head lowered, his lips brushed her slightly parted ones, allowing his tongue to coax its way into her mouth. The feel of his tongue against hers sent shivers through her body. She couldn't hold back the sigh that escaped and was immediately captured by his mouth, his large hand pressed against the small of her back to pull her closer to him. Warmth ran through her as their bodies touched. They fit perfectly, her softness meeting his hardness; the mix was exhilarating, surging her pulse to a frantic, wild rate. His arousal was evident against her, his hardness pressing against her sex, the thin material of her yoga pants little barrier between them. The grinding of his pelvis against hers, combined with the friction of her clothes just added to her arousal. The world around them ceased to exist—the birds, the waves pounding against the rocks as the storm brewed. The only thing that seemed to be present was the two of them and the heavenly feeling of his lips on hers.

Chapter Five

Gavin

Heaven. The only thought that came to his mind as his tongue tasted the flavor that was her. He had been watching her mouth as she talked, making him smile as they walked. Her pouty lips teased him, torturing him with every move. Everything about her screamed to him that she was so much more than she showed. Like there was a passion waiting just below the surface, aching to be touched—released. He knew he'd be the one to do it.

When they stopped walking, their bodies were so close, he just couldn't stop. He had to taste her, touch her, and feel her close to him. So, he just did what came naturally... he kissed her. Each touch against her skin tempted him, making his cock strain against the fabric of his jogging pants, begging to be freed, to find a place to bury itself–preferably in her. Releasing her mouth, he stepped back and met her eyes, the confusion he had assumed he would see there absent. The only thing he saw was desire.

"I hope to see you again. And maybe not when we have so little time." He stared into green eyes that sparkled like stars, as if a whole galaxy was held inside them.

With a curt nod, he turned and quickly retreated down the beach. His mind was torn. Part of him wanted to run back, push her against the wall of her home, and rip off the clothes that covered what he just knew would be a perfect body. The tank top and yoga pants she wore did hide a bit, but not too much. He could see her body curved in all the right places and was built to be loved. She wasn't a stick-and-bones kind of girl; she was a real woman. One he could really enjoy touching for hours... hell, days. Nevertheless, he kept walking; he already had a date tonight, a date with someone who might understand his needs. If he turned around and did what he wanted, he would probably scare the hell out of her, and that would ruin it for sure. Better to let her live in his fantasies.

With each step toward his home, he felt the excitement of the upcoming, well-planned event wane, the crunch of the hard sand below his feet echoing the feeling.

Was he walking away from someone he shouldn't? As if on cue, the sky above him opened up. The rain held in the dark gray clouds fell, pelting him with stinging, ice-cold drops.

"I get it. I'm the shining example of an idiot. I'm the guy who just walked away from perfection. Fuck! I didn't even get her last name!"

***

Perfectly tailored slacks lay on the bed in front of Gavin in a immaculately decorated room, the rich mahogany woodwork offset by the light sea green material on all of the bedding. He'd picked each piece decorating this room. Hours spent rummaging through catalogs, brochures, and endless piles of material swatches provided him the luxury of the rooms that felt like home. This house, like his life, was an exercise in planning. Every aspect of his day was exactly how it should be. How did he know? Because he had spent years making sure of it, not letting anything happen by mere chance. Life had shown years before that letting fate take control would leave him in a position he never wanted to be in again–hurt.

Turning toward the built-in wardrobe, he slid back the heavy door, revealing the vast assortment of shirts.

Glancing at the bedside table, he checked the color of the mask they had sent. Each participant in the masquerade would be wearing one. Gavin had opened the plain-looking white box and removed the light paper, shocked; he had never really thought of a mask as being masculine, but this one was. The dark sterling base was the color of brushed nickel. The etchings swirled throughout it were somehow rich looking. Color was minimal; a few lines of deep crimson that highlighted the mask were the only hints of it. Reviewing the shirts in front of him, he let his hand brush the material of a few of the choices. The shade had to be perfect. He was a professional at looking the part. It had made him who he was and he was not about to let that go now. Firmly tugging the shirt from the hanger, he slid it on before stepping over and placing the mask on his face to check the match. "Perfect."

Glancing at his watch, he realized he was cutting it close; the driver should be here any minute and he still had a few things to do. Rushing over to his desk, he set the mask down and typed in his access code to his laptop; instantly, the gray screen morphed into the last thing up on it. The site was still up on his screen, and he marveled at how easy it had all been. They really thought of everything. Masks, drivers, and the restaurant—not a single piece of the date had been left off, everything looked perfect. He just hoped they were this conscientious with their choice of his date.

He composed a few replies to emails that had come in during the day so far. He wanted to have nothing on his mind when he left, and this was the only way to ensure that. Unfortunately, the one thing that did not leave his mind were the red curls and matching lips of the woman he seemed to be meeting on the beach regularly now. Gavin only hoped that she would eventually fade from his thoughts tonight. It wasn't as if they would have worked anyway. She seemed entirely too sweet; definitely not the type to understand what he'd need when he brought her to his home, to his playroom, or hell, even to his bed. Even without the tools of his particular fetish, a night in his bed would take a special constitution for any woman. He did not like it easy. Well… he had never yet. "Making love," as people called it, seemed foreign to him. Hell, love did, too. It was only of late that he had seen it work, and that had given him the push to do this date. Letting his mind drift back to the conversation with his friend regarding the service, he smiled.

"You have to try it. They are amazing. It's a whole company, but really, it's Annabelle Deveroux. She is the matchmaker." Matt looked at him as he set the brandy glass down.

"And what is so special about her? Is this Annabelle one of those old women that have spent years matching couples for some Jewish community? A yenta or whatever they are called?" he asked his friend before swirling the brandy and taking a sip. "Nice, by the way. It's hard to beat the old fashioned brandy. Take this from your father's stash, did you?"

Matt laughed as he nodded his head. "You know it. The bastard always has the good stuff. No, the funny thing is Annabelle is young: our age, actually. Not Jewish, well, I don't think she is anyway. A psychologist is what I heard, and she's not married. Get that. I would have thought she would be."

Gavin looked at his friend with a quizzical, raised eyebrow. "And you want me to give her carte blanche with my life? Let her choose who I date? Hell, handle it all? You know how I am. I don't know if I can do that."

Matt placed his glass down and pointed his finger

at his friend. "Yes, I do. You of all people need this. She is good. Look at what she did for me. Now, I'm happily married. And from what I have heard, Hell did not freeze over." They both burst out laughing at that. They had always said that when either of them got married, it would have to be when Hell froze over.

"Well, maybe it's waiting for me to get married. It's just chilling now," Gavin replied in the midst of laughter as they both heard the clinking of stiletto heels coming down the hall, signaling their private moment of male bonding was definitely over.

The sound of a car horn startled him from his memories. He quickly finished his email, signed off from the computer, and picked up his mask. Securing it on his face before picking up his jacket and easing it onto his broad shoulders, he turned and headed toward the front door. As he approached, there was a gentle knock and with the turn of the knob, Gavin opened the door to find another masked man, this one in a chauffeur's uniform.

"Are you ready, Sir?"

He nodded. "Yes, thank you." Stepping out, he followed the driver as he made his way to a Town Car parked in front of his house. Sliding into the luxury car, he couldn't help but wonder who this Annabelle was and why she did all this. The woman obviously had standards—this was top of the line, for sure. But, who does this sort of thing? Turning toward the windows, he watched the scenery go by and tried his best to clear his mind.

Chapter Six

Caitlin

"Great. I have a date and my hair is being stubborn. Delightful." Her fingers were each wrapped within a curl as she did her best to tame the wild mass of hair that had been her favorite part of her physical self at times. However, today was not one of them. Today, her curls seemed to have a mind of their own, reminding her of the childhood nickname she heard for years—Medusa. "Well, that's as good as it's going to get. Hopefully it's enough." She sprayed just a bit of touchable hairspray over her hair and tucked a few butterfly-shaped diamond pins into place. The auburn hue of her locks played with the light, creating sparkles in the pins that enhanced the color. It was unique, with a rich, deep color to it that she'd never truly found on another person. She always felt tickled when people said they paid to get the color she had naturally.

She picked up the black dress that she had hung on the bathroom door while she showered, keeping the fan off to allow a deluge of steam to be caught in the room, steaming the dress to perfection. Unfortunately, she had not thought that she would be doing this, and her house here definitely not stocked for dates. She didn't have a multitude of choices; most of her beach wardrobe was filled with knit pants and comfy tee shirts or tanks. A few casual dresses, mostly knit, were the highlight of the selection. Tucked away in the back of the closet she had found this one dress, and it was going to have to do. It had been a joke really that it even came.

She remembered packing it up a few visits prior, convincing herself that she was going to find some nice place to go, maybe a club or something, and would need the dress. That had never happened; there were no nice clubs on the coast, instead, she had walked into the one club she had found in Newport and immediately turned around and went home. Everyone was in jeans and casual shirts, and some looked like they had literally just come in off a boat. The dress had sat after that and each trip had been pushed further and further into a dark corner. Casual days laying around on the beach, perusing around the local shops of the

60

little beach town… That she had the necessary clothes for, but not a date. Luckily, she had the one dress. Not the one she would have originally chosen, but it would work. She stepped into the silky black material and felt the softness of the garment sliding up her body. The light material fell against her breasts, laying perfectly in the cleavage, exposing the top of her ample breasts, yet hugged her hips to accentuate the natural curve of her waistline.

She was proud of her body, worked at it constantly. She was not a tiny girl. At one point in her life she had been, but then one day, her metabolism had changed, and from that day forward, it had been a daily struggle to stay in a size ten. Her height had always been a savior; most people would never guess what she weighed or the size of her clothing. She carried it well in her opinion. Deep down, she always wondered if her weight was part of the reason she was alone. That a man would never really want to stay with a girl like her, a bit more girl than they bargained for. If what they really wanted was that small girl who would look good at the parties, all cute and perfect, not curvy and smart.

Stepping over to the standing mirror in the corner of her bedroom, Caitlin smoothed the material over her hips, making sure that every inch hung just the right way. As she came to the top of the dress she let her fingers glide over the drop of the material in the front where it fell just between her supple breasts. Well-endowed, she never had to worry about not having enough. Finding clothes that fit right and didn't make her look like she was trying out for strip club, with her D-cup breasts on full display, was hard. Pulling the material to the right just a tad, she made sure it fit properly and didn't look as if she were falling out of the dress.

The tick of the clock on the wall got her attention, and she realized that the driver would be here any moment. Picking up the necklace that she'd set out earlier, the silver chain shone as she placed it against her skin. The ruby glowed in the light of the room and matched her hair perfectly. Taking a quick turn in front of the mirror, she smiled. "Well, I like it. I would totally date me."

"That's the spirit."

She whirled around at the sound of Sarah's voice. "What do you think?"

Sarah just nodded and walked around her in a small circle. "Perfect. He is going to be drooling."

She heard the crunch of tires outside and quickly hugged her friend loosely so she wouldn't wreck her makeup or hair, then slipped on black stiletto slingbacks and headed to the door. As she opened it, the driver was just coming up the stairs. She saw his eyes widen as she stepped out.

"Hi. You're here for me." The driver looked her up and down, and she started to feel a bit uncomfortable when he didn't say anything, just stared at her wistfully. Just when she was ready to consider calling the whole thing off, he pulled out a small box from his coat pocket.

"Yes, I am here for you. And this is for you."

She took the silver box and lifted the light cover, her hands shaking ever so slightly as her nerves got the best of her. "Thank you."

The filmy whiteness of the paper inside looked so clean it could have been made from fresh snow. And as she pulled it from the top, a small gasp escaped her. "Oh my, this is beautiful!" The black mask was simple yet beautiful. She held it up, admiring the workmanship. It was obviously expensive, and she felt decadent as she held it up to her face. "Would you mind? I can't hold this up and tie it."

63

The driver took a minute to respond, and then as if it were a hardship, he nodded his head and stepped behind her. Feeling the silk ties come tight against her, his fingers gently moved a lock of hair out of the way. Again, that feeling of unease clambered up inside her, her stomach turning just a bit from nerves.

"Thank you."

The only response she got was a single nod, then he held his hand held out, directing her toward the car. She took a step forward and the man cut in front, beating her to the car and pulling open the door.

Silently, she slid in and looked around. The seats were plush leather, the color of onyx, the inside walls inlaid with deep cherry wood, giving it a look of luxury. A bottle of champagne had been set to chill and a glass sat waiting. Thinking there was nothing better to help with her nervous stomach than a glass, she quickly poured some and sat back as the car pulled out of the driveway and headed into the night. Every few minutes, she felt eyes watching her and after the fourth time, she caught him, pushing the button to raise the privacy glass. Caitlin didn't know if it was normal or not, but the way the man looked at her sent shivers down her spine and a nervous roll through her stomach. Settling back in the plush seat, she took a sip of her drink while gazing out the window, knowing that tonight was a whim, a fantasy creation. More than likely, she was not going to be coming home with someone. Tomorrow, just like this morning and every one before it, she would probably wake up alone, with no prospect of a man in her life.

Chapter Seven

Gavin

Gavin sat back against the deeply cushioned, burgundy-upholstered chair, his eyes drawn from the golden flicker of the flame dancing atop the candle to the crackling of the fire warming the room; no one else was there, obviously the place had been rented for the evening. There was only one table in the room, set just for them; their own private space. The rich burgundy walls highlighted the flame's light, giving off the feeling of utter decadence.

He picked up the envelope from the table with his name on it. Opening the thick golden envelope, he pulled the filmy paper out to read the perfectly scrawled writing.

"This is your night, everything is yours,
and yours alone; there are no other
restaurant guests and even the staff
has been hand-picked for your privacy,
so have no fear.
A night for two.
There is a key in the car for when dinner
is done if you need a space to retreat to,
set up just as you would have it yourself,
I am sure.
Enjoy!
-Annabelle"

Placing the envelope in his inside jacket pocket, he smiled knowingly. Oh, Annabelle knew exactly what he liked. More so than most. If she said it was set, it was set. This space was proof of that.

Soft piano music heightened the ambiance of the room, coming from nowhere in particular; not a single speaker was visible to the naked eye, and the music seemed to come from everywhere. His fingers grazed over the dark tablecloth, and he shivered as he felt the change in the temperature, as if a wind had blown in from the cold world outside this safe cocoon.

Gazing toward the entry, his stomach twisted just a bit and his breath caught in his throat. *"Stunning beauty"*: those were the only words that came to mind as his vision trailed over her, his mind instantly going to the old saying his grandmother used to tell him as a young boy. "It's always better when something is left to the imagination." Right now, he had to agree with that. The silky black fabric of her dress clung to just the right places, leaving a bit of skin exposed to his eyes; God, there was a part of him that wanted to be that dress, to see and feel what was covered so well by the layers of silk that surrounded her. Everything was covered, but he was willing to bet that under that silken cover was the softest skin. Her face was perfect, that he could see. The mask she wore covered most of it, but her lips were plump, inviting, the kind that begged to have lips against them. As she moved closer, he pushed back his chair and slowly rose out of his seat, walking over to hers and pulling it back just enough.

"Hello. You look lovely."

He watched her eyes drop to the floor as well as the

subtle nod of her head.

"Hello."

Her voice. Something about it stirred something deep inside him. He did not know what, but something was there. As she sat in the chair he held out, the scent of her hit him, his body tightening in response—so delectable. Taking a steadying breath, he went back to his seat directly opposite her. *Not the most talkative.* Expectations of some talkative little bimbo had originally been his fear. It was pleasant to find that this was not the case, but now a new worry took its place. What if she was not interested in him or, worse yet, him in her? The thought sent chills down his back. He was running out of ideas or hopes to find "the one." The silence as they sat there watching each other was deafening. He knew someone had to start the conversation or this was going nowhere quickly. He sat, wishing that this date were really with the girl from the beach. They had fallen so easy into conversation. Nevertheless, he knew the likelihood that things would work with someone he met on his own was slim to none.

"So, is this your first time using the agency?"

Her eyes finally rose from the table and he fought

the urge to reach up and rip off the mask; something about her eyes seemed so familiar. The waiter appeared, breaking the awkwardness as he delivered appetizers and filled their glasses. Picking up the champagne flute, he raised his toward her.

"To us and a new beginning." The smile that graced her lips was magnificent, and he couldn't help but smile in return.

"To us." Her voice so melodic, something about it soothed him.

As they progressed through dinner, he did his best to get her to speak, and each answer was one or two words. No more. When dessert came, he knew he had to do something or this would just be a waste of time.

"I know this is different. What made you do it?" As he waited, the minutes crawled by. Just about to put down the little spoon, her voice penetrated the quiet.

"I don't know who is real anymore. My relationships in the past have always started well, and then they just fizzled out. They have always left. I just wanted someone…"

70

The pause in her sentence, combined with the way her whole body sagged for that one second, was as if she dropped the guard placed around he. It spoke to him, and he forced himself to fight the desire to rush to her side of the table and take her in, fought the overwhelming need to vow to protect her from whatever she was afraid of, from anything that would hurt her.

"…Someone who was willing to ride the tides of life with me. Not just the good times, but the others as well. I need something… someone different, who is not afraid of being them, of being different. I am always in complete control. Everything in its place. But now… I'm tired."

He sat stunned for a minute or two as he listened to her. "You're very beautiful, I cannot even fathom you having any issues finding someone."

Her head fell back and she laughed; the sound, he was sure, the same as angels in heaven when they laughed.

"Thank you. Unfortunately, that is not as true as you would think. I am in no means disillusioned about who or what I am. I am not a model by any means, and as you can see by my empty plate, I do love my food. Unfortunately, I also love a man to be a man, to be who I

71

imagine him to be. Which is probably because I read too many romance novels growing up."

He laughed gently as she babbled on about her desires. Each desire she mentioned matched with one he had to give but had never ever found a woman that really wanted it. They both finished eating and, pushing back from the table, he stood and came around to her side to hold out his hand to the lovely woman.

"Walk with me, will you?" The minute her hand touched his, he felt a tingle of electricity run through him. He watched the firelight sparkle off her auburn curls that swayed as she moved. She was perfect, and he had a hunch she was more than she said. Much more.

Chapter Eight

Caitlin

All through dinner, she did her best to keep control. His voice sent chills through her. This made two men in one week with that deep voice that just oozed sexuality. She would be perfectly happy to listen to him speak for hours. Her body came alive for it. She was sure that when she stood, a wet spot would show on her dress, and that would be mortifying. As she took his hand, she felt a tingle of anticipation. Just the idea of touching this man sent shivers down her spine; the thought of letting her hand skim up his chest, well, that was just going to give her a heart attack, she was sure.

When she stood in front of him, she felt his eyes heating her from the inside out. Her breasts started to tingle, her nipples tightened, teasing against the lace of her bra, and her sex started to throb. Moisture now became very evident as it reached the soft skin of her thigh. Then, in one swift movement, he reached his hand around her, cradling her head at the base and pulling her to him, claiming her lips with his. His tongue invaded her mouth as she let out a gasp at the surprise of the pull of her body to his. Raising her hands and pressing them against his firm chest, she could feel the definition of his muscles, despite the fact that he was fully dressed. The fight in her left as his tongue swirled around hers, brushing against hers, coaxing it to his. When his tongue started to recede, she sucked it gently, not wanting to let it go, a moan escaping her.

Stars. Her head felt as if it were swirling, the world around her spiraling; she could have been flying for all she knew. His hand held her firmly. She dared not move, as he forbid it. The force of his hand told her so. No question. The feeling of his hand on her lower back, slowly sliding down, running along the open back of her dress over her rounded curves sent shivers down her spine. When he finally released her mouth, she tipped her head up to look into his eyes. Instantly, fear rocked her. His eyes plainly showed his desire, there swirling in the depths. She could see, hell, *feel* his want, but she didn't know if she could really give what was so plainly in his eyes. Was she even capable of being

74

that wanted girl? Of giving herself freely to him? Would she be able to protect herself? Her heart? What if he thought he wanted her and then didn't?

"You are so soft." His voice was so final; there was no question in his words, just statements of fact, which scared her yet turned her on. "Come with me. I have a place we can go. Be mine for tonight."

His words hit her like a cold shower. This was real. He was exactly what she wanted. This was not some fairy tale, this was the real world, and everything she did had an effect. It would be so easy to let her guard down, to give in, and give herself to him. The thought scared her to death. Every past failure, every heartbreak rushed to her mind. This was different, just the barest touch of his hand had told her that; sparks between them was an understatement. Quickly, she pulled away and ran toward the door that led to her freedom. Fear propelled her as she opened it and looked back to him with a lowered head. "I am so sorry. I just can't."

Throwing herself out the door of the restaurant and down the stairs, she saw her driver jump out of the car's front door and open her door. Before the man could make his way around to her side of the car, she had already climbed in, slammed the door, put up the privacy glass, and started crying silently. Tears streamed down her face, moist trails holding her dreams of what could have been. Yes, dinner was great, but if she had taken that step and followed him, then things became real, life changing, and so many repercussions could result. More than she was ready to give or receive. Because if fantasy became reality and that failed, then what did she have? Her last hope and dream would be gone. Her life would have no more to feed it. No more dreams to get through the winter nights, not more fantasy. Nothing.

When the car started, she just fell further back into the seat and as the miles went by, her tears flowed, taking her hope away with it.

The car stopping caused her to raise her head from its perch on her hands. When the door opened, she flung herself through the opening and ran up the stairs to her home. Safely inside, she let the tears and sobs fall across the empty rooms, her sorrow and fear taking complete control of her... and her future. Making her way to her bedroom, she dropped her purse on the floor and sighed before falling onto the bed. Everything she had thought she wanted had been there. He was perfect, they had been perfect—they would have been perfect. They could talk, really get along outside of the bedroom. Even with just the kiss, the mind-blowing all-consuming kiss, she knew that the bedroom would have been spectacular. But he knew her, somehow he did, with the way he controlled her by just a kiss and the barest of touches. She would have no escape if it went bad. He could see her soul. That scared her most of all. He could get through her walls—and truly hurt her.

Chapter Nine

Gavin

Three Weeks Later

Gavin stared out the window of his home; weeks had gone by since he had gone on that date, yet he could not get past her. Contracts sat in front of him; in the past contracts used to keep him riveted to his work, now they did nothing for him. His partners were starting to worry, each making appearances at his office door saying they were concerned, until it was just easier for him to go home and work from there. Who was she, they would ask; the problem was he knew everything about her was good, sexy. She was submissive naturally: her body language, her answers to all his questions had told him that, and yet he did not even know who she was for sure. Something about her had called to him. She was so passionate, the way she responded to his kiss and the way her body had molded to his so perfect.

The agency had called and apologized profusely to him, offering him a complete refund for the money he had paid for their services. They swore they would not stop looking for other dates for him, even if it took them around the world to find a good match. Apparently he had broken the mold. None of their past clients had ever encountered this type of problem. His mind went back to the drive away from the Oregon Coast, it had been the longest one he had made, but the beach no longer held the peace he needed. Now it held the woman he wanted, the one that haunted his mind... his very soul. Turning from the window, he grabbed his keys off the oak desk and headed to his car to drive to work.

***

His phone rang the minute he walked into his office. The fact Gavin had made it through the reception area with out an inquisition truly was proof of a higher power. He probably scared them all away with the sour grimace on his face; no one in the glass enclosed space took more than a second's glance, each would look then immediately dart their eyes, some shuffling papers, others just plainly heading in the opposite direction. No stops on the way through the hall put him pushing open the heavy oak door to his private office in record time. The space before him was modern, with sleek lines, highlighted by a glass wall that overlooked the Seattle skyline. The gray clouds that filled the sky were a match to his mood. The large chair tucked under the larger desk slid out easily; with a heavy sigh he sat down, pulled the chair in, pushed the round button on the laptop. Two quick rings on the phone, the sound that signaled it was an internal caller, brought his attention from the laptop. Looking at his caller ID, his stomach lurched before he picked up the phone.

"Gavin here." He looked aimlessly over the piles of messages on his desk as he listened to Shelly.

"Yes sir, we thought you should know there has been a development on the search for a model for the latest campaign. The client has someone they want to use, but the model has an exclusivity contract. We would need to speak with the model's attorney. Did you want me to handle it?"

He pulled out a blank sheet of paper, grabbing his pen from his pocket. "No, I will. I need to get back into the swing of things. Thank you, by the way, for taking care of so much." He heard Shelly sigh in the background, apparently not happy.

"It's no problem. I just think you need to take some more time off. I really don't know what happened, and I am not asking to know, far be it that I pry into your life like you do mine, but you're not you. Don't take that wrong, but you actually have said please to me a number of times. Let me tell you… that is, well, just not you, not that I mind really. But."

He interrupted her. "Thanks. I got it. Now what is the model's attorney's name?" His pen flew across the page as he wrote out the name—Caitlin Leeway.

"Thanks, Shelly. I will give her a call." He hung up the phone, immediately turning to his laptop. Gavin quickly typed in the address bar and up popped Google. Making his way to the local bar association information page, he proceeded to type in her name; the bio immediately came up. The place for a picture showed nothing, but her bio was very informative. A young, up-and-coming attorney, top in her field, which made no sense at all as her field was family law, not entertainment law. The sigh escaped his lips in a rush; dammit, he didn't need to be that asshole boss.

Realizing he was a bit rash with Shelly only

moments ago he thought through it again; she had always been nice, truly caring to him, plus she was right. More than one time he had intruded in her life, when a boyfriend or friend was taking advantage of her, stepping in to play that big brother role. Really, she was spot on.

"Work... Work..."

Gavin processed through the reasons a family attorney would be involved at all in this deal, and came up with nothing. His client said an exclusivity contract but this attorney's field was family law, definitely not contract law, not entertainment, not anything remotely related to what this model would need. Pushing the button on his phone that rang the extension of his assistant, he heard her breathe before she spoke.

"You said Caitlin Leeway, correct?" He tried to make sure his voice came across calm and in control.

"Yep, that's the one. Family friend or something," Shelly said in a quipped tone.

Family friend, well that explains that, make more sense at least, he thought.

"Thanks, sorry for biting your head off earlier. Just

a lot going on."

Pushing the release button on the phone, he took one more chance to look over the contract on his desk along with the profile still up on his laptop. After just a moment's thought, he rolled his large black leather chair back from the desk and grasped his keys. He did not like to do business over the phone, especially when it was on a contract that was capable of bringing in a million dollars easily. His best bet was a personal visit to her office. Jotting down the address, which was just across town, he made his way out of his office, only stopping to let Shelly know where he was going to be, before he retreated back down the twelve floors to the garage below.

Chapter Ten

Caitlin

Work had been her solace after crying all night and dwelling on the fact that she had probably thrown away the one good thing that had happened to her since, well, as long as she could remember. Past boyfriends, all gone, her family, well, they might as well be gone. She was for all intents and purposes on the far side of the glass watching her family. It wouldn't matter if she wrote letters, begged for conversation, or said hey I am so sorry for not being everything you ever wanted in a child, she would be ignored. Hell, any letter would have been returned to sender, of that she had no doubt. Her mind replayed the visit from her mother just days before she had headed down to Oregon.

Maryanne Johnson, as she currently was known, had waltzed into Caitlin's office after completely insulting the reception staff. "You really should have your own firm by now, darling. I mean, if you're going to insist on doing this whole career thing." Caitlin had lifted her head from her legal briefs and stared at the whirlwind that was her mother.

"Hello, Mom." Well, I wonder what I did now to deserve a personal appearance, *she thought. "Sorry you had to come down; I can tell it's trying on your nerves. What did you need?"*

The tall blonde spun on the balls of her pointed five-inch heeled pumps and sat down on the plush chair in front of Caitlin's desk as if it was a park bench covered in dirt, almost as if she was trying to hover over it so she wouldn't get dirty.

"I received a call from Michael's mother. I assumed you had maybe taken some time to realize that you were making another stupid mistake and were ready to beg for his forgiveness. I think I can convince him, with the help of his mother, to take you back. You will have to make some concessions, of course. Like quit the childish game you have going here and become the wife he needs. You will, of course, marry him."

Caitlin almost stood up and screamed but instead her mother's words just numbed her.

"Look mom, he doesn't want me back and really I don't want him back. Moreover, I cannot be what he wants and this is not childish. This is my world. You do not have to be a part of it. You walked in here." She kept her eyes on her mother's, not wanting to give in, not wanting to show weakness. If she did... it was over.

"Obviously I thought you were ready to be my daughter.... Not this... working girl." Her mother's sneer at the working girl comment wasn't missed as she looked her daughter over with a look of complete distaste. "But you're right. I did walk in here, because I thought you were ready, and wanted to be part of the society and life that I fought for you to have. But no, you have to just sit there and throw it all away. Well, this I can fix. I will be walking out that door and I will not be walking back. Goodbye, Caitlin."

Caitlin held her head up, and did her very best to hold her tears in until she heard the click of the lock on the door. Only then did she let the tears fall. She was alone. Again.

Her hands worked through the items piled in front

of her on the bed. Each piece was folded perfectly; the benefit of single life, she thought as she took one of the shirts and messed it up before shoving it back inside the bag. Caitlin stared down at the faded pink t-shirt before pulling it back out, refolding it, and putting it back in neatly. Ok, it was nice she could do anything she wanted, but really, who was she lying to? Herself? Not worth it. As she continued packing her things, she looked up at the doorframe and smiled at her friend, who had apparently snuck in the room.

"Look, here you go." She handed the keys to the beach house to Sarah.

"You sure?" The questioning tone did not go unnoticed.

"Yes, I'm sure. You can stay as long as you want. Just make sure to cover the furniture outside before you leave and lock it all up tight. Then take the keys to Stacy down the way. Oh and please, make sure not to leave food in the fridge. I don't want to come back to that smell."

"Great avoidance there…." Sarah quipped.

"Learned from years of practice; now, I'm gone."

She gave Sarah a hug, picked up her bag, heading for the door.

During the drive to Seattle, her mind ran through the conversation she had that morning with Stacy, her friend from down the beach. Sarah had called her, she was sure of it, almost as if she was bringing in reinforcements.

"You here?"

She had pushed up from the bed at the sound of her neighbor coming through the door. "In here." She sat up and waited. When her bedroom door opened, a very pregnant Stacy waddled in and plopped herself down on the bed.

"Okay, what's up? You look like a mess and you should be blissfully happy, content in the glow of spectacular sex; plus, Sarah called and said you were turtled in your room."

She nodded. "Yes, you would think that, but no, he was great, but he was too much."

"You mean too human? Wanted you to be, you know, real too?"

"Stop, Stacy. I am real, but he would have left. Better off not finding myself attached, and I could with someone like him. He literally made me want him in about five minutes. Serious."

"Damn, I would love that. Got his number? Maybe he likes preggo girls."

Caitlin smacked Stacy with a pillow. "No, you can't call him."

"Well, I just came by to tell you I am in control of the house when you leave today. I got your text, so it's all good. When Sarah leaves the keys with me, I will do the usual—water the plants, let the cleaning people in, watch the landscape company... yada, yada. But I'm serious. You need to stop running and let someone in. You won't regret it."

Caitlin stood up and stretched, then walked toward the kitchen, the sound of Stacy waddling behind her comforting her to some degree; she wasn't alone and Stacy always felt like a mommy of sorts to her despite their close age difference.

"You mean stop running like you did? You still feel

that way, despite the fact you're left to raise a baby by yourself, while the babe's father gallivants around the world? I still don't know why you won't let me go after him for child support."

"Yes, I do still feel this way. And no, you may not go after him. You see, even if it was just for a short while, I found release...true happiness. He will come back. He is just pulling a, well—you. Running from the life he could have, the family. When he is ready, he will come home. His daughter and I will be waiting. Now, I have to run. Love you."

***

"Come in." Caitlin's assistant Vivian tripped as she walked in, and Caitlin couldn't help but roll her eyes; Vivian was always a bull in a china closet. If it was breakable she would break it; tippable? It would crash and shatter; yet, when it came to research the girl was unbeatable.

"Yes, you know you could have just pressed that little button on your phone and said whatever. You don't have to come in here, especially if you can't manage the whole walking thing." She saw the hurt look in the eyes of
90

the woman standing in front of her. "I'm sorry. I don't know what came over me. I am so sorry. You don't deserve it."

Vivian smiled timidly before she looked up. "I came to tell you that someone is here to see you. About a client of yours."

"Which client?" She became slightly annoyed having to ask but forged forward.

"Oh, I forgot to ask."

Setting her pencil down, she sat back against the plush leather chair. "Fine, just send them in."

Vivian quickly left the room leaving the door open on her way out, and Caitlin took the minute before whoever was coming made their way in to finish what she was working on. She just needed to find that one line…

She rifled through the papers neatly pilled on her desk. The firm click of the door closing echoed around the large, sparsely decorated office, catching her attention. She looked up and smiled. Pushing from the chair, she stood and held out her hand to a stunning specimen of a man. Tall and handsome, instantly her heart caught in her chest.

"Hello again. It looks like fate is finally going to introduce us. Officially, that is. I'm Caitlin Leeway. How can I help you?"

Fuck, it's the man from the beach. The kisser. How the hell did this happen? She'd been doing everything to forget the beach, which in itself was not the usual. Fate or whoever controlled things was definitely into cruelty; she was being thrown into a walking, talking memory.

"Well, you could help me arrange for one of your clients to be the model for my latest campaign. In case you don't remember me, I'm Gavin, Gavin McDonald." He grasped her hand in a firm shake.

She threw her head back and laughed as she dropped his hand.

"I like you. Right to the point." She looked down at her watch and smiled. "Well, it's lunch time. What do you say we have this discussion over lunch?" She knew she was completely using him. He reminded her of *him*: same height, same build, same all-consuming aura, just like the mystery man from the date. Just being near him made her feel protected, much like the feeling she had that fateful night.

92

"Sure. Sounds good to me. I know a Greek place in Fremont, just past the bridge. Great food, great views. Here, let me get the door." He held it open, and she grasped her clutch; his hand landed on the small of her back, the warmth seeping right through her blouse as she walked through the exit, a gesture she did not miss, and one that sent her skin on a ride through what felt like the center of the earth from the heat.

Annoying music filled the elevator as they made their way down to the ground floor. When the heavy steel gray door slid open she strode through.

"My car is in the garage. Did you want to meet me there or ride with me?" His smile made her breath catch. How was it possible that he was even more attractive? "Call me old-fashioned but I like to drive when taking a lady to lunch. This way. My car is right out front." His hand beckoned and she couldn't help but comply. It was not a question; it was a statement. A directive and God, she liked that. The walk to his car was quick; he had been honest, it was right out the door. And in seconds he was opening the door and she was sliding inside, making sure that the skirt she was wearing didn't ride up too high.

"Thank you," she said as he went to close the door.

"You're welcome." Then he closed the door.

The drive held views of bustling crowds waiting for buses along with throngs of cars waiting for one light or another, making up the life of downtown Seattle. Caitlin felt calm, almost comfortable. She knew it had to be the feeling of him there, that he felt, well, natural around her.

"How long have you lived here? I have been here forever, it feels, yet I don't think I have ever met you before, except for on the beach hundreds of miles away."

He looked at her as she questioned him. "Grew up in Olympia actually, moved up here after I came back from college, just close enough to get home when I wanted to, yet far enough away that my family have to call to visit." His laugh was so sincere she couldn't help but relax a bit.

"I understand completely. I was raised on the Oregon Coast, moved up here to Seattle for college and just never went back."

"University of Washington?"

"Yes. Go Huskies." She pumped her fist in the air

as if holding a pom-pom. She stepped out of his car as they parked close to The Troll, the giant troll carved into the dirt underground of the bridge, his big hand holding an actual VW Bug, smiling when she realized he had tried to get around to her side of the car before she got out, but she had been quicker. Turning toward the troll sculpture, she pointed. "What do you think they made him for? I mean really?"

Gavin smiled at her and her body warmed. He was so easy to talk to. The conversation should have been all business, but she couldn't do it. Maybe it was the fact she had met him at the beach, but her relaxed side, the one that only came out at the beach was making an appearance in the city—a space that was usually filled with the side with no personality, no fun, just what she could achieve career-wise.

"Well, historians and locals say it was a statement about not wanting the Californians to move in. However, I personally like the other popular belief that others swear by, that it's all about *The Three Billy Goats Gruff*. Call me a kid at heart, but I like it."

She laughed. Her heart felt light and she smiled, which she had not done in weeks.

Caitlin watched as he held his hand out to her, almost stopping her heart. The last time someone had done that, the gesture had included an invitation, one that had scared her to hell. Now, she was not afraid, maybe because he was just so normal, so casual, and so easy. This time, she saw her hand moving almost as if she watched as someone else controlled her hand. When her small palm landed in his large one, a tingle went through her body.

"Lunch then?" His deep voice reverberated through her.

She nodded and they started walking, hand in hand, down the hill toward the river. It was something she had not done in years: walked through the city, no deadline, no meeting demanding where she went, just walked and enjoyed the city she lived in. They stopped and pointed at items in the windows, laughing and making small talk.

When they reached the bright blue door of Costa Opa's, his hand rested on the small of her back, and she did her best to not react as her heart did—stopping short. She smiled and waited as he opened the door, then led her through with just the gentlest pressure. The hostess greeted them, her peppy smile almost sickening, but Caitlin knew it was simply her job. Gavin let her take the lead, and she set out following the perfectly sized brunette. *Great, another shining example of perfection, something I never will be*, Caitlin grumbled in her head. Stopping at the table in the far corner, she immediately went to pull out a chair and sit down when Gavin came up behind her and his hand reached the chair before hers, holding it out like some romance movie. Struck by how completely sweet it was, she could not help but smile.

"Thank you," she said, as she sat down and he scooted her forward gently.

"You're welcome. Now, what should we order? I don't know about you, but I love their flaming cheese."

She looked up at him as he finished getting himself settled on his side. "The what?" *God, he must be crazy*, she thought, laughing gently.

"Saganaki is the I guess real name of it but I just like calling it flaming cheese, seriously one of my favorites. And they do it so well here."

Watching him fascinated her. She was mesmerized by his confidence, his complete sureness at being himself.

He showed no visible doubt. It was comforting, something she wished she could have. Hell, she was so far from confident she was the poster child for insecurity. Sometimes she could picture a blinking sign above her head with the word "nuts" on it.

"Caitlin?" His soothing voice focused her attention back on the here and now.

"Oh, I am so sorry, yes, let's get that. Might as well try it. I always say I'll try anything once."

"Really? Anything?" He smiled at her, a twinkle in his eyes along with heavy eyelids that drooped seductively as they looked at her, causing her breath to hitch.

"Yes. And today's new thing is cheese."

Chapter Eleven

Gavin

Innocent and timid. That was what he thought of the woman in front of him. Yet he had done his research and she was not timid. All he knew was that he had been given a chance to see those perfect lips and stunning eyes one more time, and he was going to draw this out as long as he could. Contract be damned, he was not going to just let this be a business lunch. He wanted more.

When the waitress brought the flaming dish, he watched Caitlin's eyes glisten and dance with excitement at the little flames before they were put out. There was so much life in her, he could tell. But when she noticed him looking, a virtual wall quickly slammed down in place, the business-like seriousness reappearing. He was going to find his way through that wall, break it down, and then see what lay behind it.

Gavin watched as she took her first bite, the way her eyes closed as the fork brought the little bit of cheese to her lips. Fighting the urge to reach under the table and adjust himself as he felt the snugness of his pants increase as her plump lips closed around the fork. His mind instantly wished his cock was that fork, feeling her lips close around him. Over and over the processes repeated; the only reason he even made it through the meal without causing a scene and being arrested for lewd behavior was the distraction his own meal and the pleasant conversation supplied him.

"Well? You liked it, right?" He smiled as he watched her place her blue cloth napkin on her plate.

"God yes. This was the best Greek food I have had in years!"

He noticed her hand move as she reached toward the bill, and he quickly grasped the leather portfolio. "Nope, not going to happen. This one is on me. Again, I'm old-fashioned like that. Pampering my dates and spoiling them is my prerogative." Placing his black Amex in the folder, he held it up for the waitress who made her way over.

"This was not a date. This was business," she said, shocked.

"I beg to differ. We didn't even talk about the exclusivity contract for the ad. But I know your favorite color and your love of the area." He watched her thinking, practically seeing the wheels turning in her head. Pushing back from the table, he held out his hand to her.

"Shall we?"

Her nod was subtle as she rose and slowly put her hand in his, and then quickly removed it. "Sorry."

"Don't be." He guided her toward the door with his hand on her back. Part of him desperately wanted to let his hand slide down toward her perfectly sculpted ass, but knew that would be the wrong thing to do. Hell, he wanted to have her to himself, not share her with the city. He had fantasized about her for weeks. Well, between her and the mystery woman from that night; in his dreams, they had become interchangeable. Why? He had no clue, and now that they were again walking through the crowds on the Fremont streets, he was finally feeling like he could get past the disaster of that night at the beach.

"Caitlin, I know you don't think this was a date, and I will give you that, but you have to give me something in exchange."

She looked up at him, his eyes mesmerized by the gold specks in her green eyes that caught the sunlight as it streamed between the buildings.

"Well, what do you have in mind? If it's the contract signed, send it to my office, and I am sure we can make that happen."

Shaking his head gently just before he stopped in front of the Volkswagen Beetle covered by the big hand of The Troll "Nope. Not what I want."

"Really? What do you want? I thought work was what this was all about."

"Oh, you're right, I do want the model for my client, but I want something more... something a bit more personal. I want you."

Chapter Twelve

Caitlin

"Me?" Her body flared, heat racing through her, bringing parts to life that she had last felt that night at the restaurant. She remembered the feel of his kiss that day at the beach—the way it made her feel, the want, and the desire. He was so down-to-earth, so easy to talk to, so—safe. Taking a deep breath and centering herself, she put on her best I-am-so-calm-and-collected-and-sure-of-myself look and smiled. "Well then, I guess you should pick me up at seven on Friday. But first, I need a ride to my office."

She smiled as she walked to the car and saw the lights flash as he unlocked the car, then grasped the door and she climbed in. She had to keep busy, keep moving, anything to keep him from seeing that this sure of herself façade was just that: a façade. Inside she was ready to throw up, her stomach was rolling, and her mind was racing. She had seen him at the beach, he had been oh-so-sexy and everything she could have wanted in a relationship, except one. What if he was just that perfect friend, not the oh yeah baby she was looking for? The toe curling, pussy clenching, heat inducing man that would come into her life and not just whisk her off her feet but slam her against the wall and remind her she was a woman.

"That sounds perfect for a normal date. But since we just had our first date–" He put his hand up to block her from stopping him, cutting off her whole rebuttal before she even started. "I have a better idea."

He drove them back to her office, deftly avoiding the buses that stopped randomly and the pedestrians that were as usual not bothering to stay on the sidewalks or crosswalks as they made their way to the Pike Place Market. Pulling up to the front of her building, he reached behind her seat, his body so close to hers that she could smell his very manly scent—a heady mix of cologne and man, a smell that never, ever failed to get her pulse racing. He rifled through a briefcase behind her before pulling back, holding out a small, off-white card.

"What's this?" She looked at the small business

card.

"This is my other idea. My address—my very private address—to my home in the city. Moreover, *you* should be there at 7 p.m. prepared to have the meal of your dreams. I have other skills, you know, other than small talk and beach walking. I can cook. Oh... and wear casual clothes... Nothing fancy."

Caitlin laughed, truly laughed, her head thrown back as she saw the playful look in his eyes, as if he was someone who showed that side regularly. "Fine. I will see you Friday. You have a date." She got out of the car, waving before turning and heading into her building, every insecurity attacking her as she walked. Rushing into the elevator, she fought the urge to pass out. Her world spiraled around her, heart pounding in her chest as everything around her amplified. The voices of the others in the elevator became louder while the walls felt as if they were closing in on her, and anxiety seized her. The elevator pings were gongs, and when it arrived at her floor, the heavy steel doors slid open with a deafening whoosh. Practically throwing people out of her way, she rushed through the opening and raced down the hall to her office. Finally safe, she shoved the door closed and fell onto the couch on the far side of the room.

"What have I done? It was supposed to be business. What the hell have I done?"

***

Friday night Caitlin looked toward her open closet. All her clothes were hanging, each item exactly half an inch from the next, all the colors lined up perfectly, starting with the solids and cascading over to patterns with that color before moving to the next solid color. Everything had been precisely arranged, color-coded, and set by use. They were perfect, giving her a moment of peace inside because the world around her was now spinning. She had no idea why she had agreed to this. Yes, it was nice to spend time with him, or it had been. And wow, talk about chemistry, but was that enough? She stood up from the plush burgundy round stool, handpicked at the flea market years ago. Back when she could not afford half the clothes that now hung around her, Caitlin looked around at the mess that was dozens of outfits discarded as not what she was looking for, now waiting for her to pick them back up and put them away.

"You are okay," she said to herself. Picking up the

cell phone, she dialed Sarah, the keys lightly beeping as she hit each number.

"Panic attack?" Sarah's voice came through clear as could be.

"How did you know?" Caitlin started pacing around the room.

"Well, the same way I know you're going back and forth from your closet, making track marks that you will eventually have to vacuum away so you won't see the treads of your feet. Because that, too, will drive you incredibly nuts. I used to walk across the living room of our apartment just to piss you off, you know."

"Seriously? I knew it. I couldn't believe you really needed to go in there right after I'd cleaned."

"See, you're breathing again. Now, tell me what's up."

Caitlin sighed and sat down on her bed. "What am I doing, Sarah?" She hung her head, bracing it on her palm.

"Well, you're going to put on a nice pair of jeans and a nice low-cut top, or maybe a little black dress. It's not your first date."

"Yes, I know, but this is him, and he did say casual."

"Tall, bald, built, and beach. Yes, I know. He is your fantasy. Nevertheless, you need to do this. I had given up hope, resigned myself to being your 'plus one' forever."

"You know my office, all the work that it creates and my contracts are great; hell, divorce is easier than this."

Caitlin heard the sigh through the phone as she finished her sentence. "Yes, and you will only have the office, your contracts, and the end of marriages if you do not go. Did you ever stop to think that you are in family law because its easier to watch families fall apart than to think of them succeeding? You didn't have love when you were young, your adult relationships are not really a great story; I get it. But you need to do this. You deserve to have a bit of the fantasy, your fairy tale. Now get going, and call me when you get home."

Damn, she was so freaking right all the time.

"Fine, I'm going." Hanging up, she made her way into the closet, giving up and just picking out clothes, comfortable ones for the night. Happy with her choices, as the spaghetti strap black tank top and blue jeans paired perfectly with the black ballet flats, she stood in front of the floor-length mirror going over the complete look; unable to imagine why Gavin would be interested in her. Hell, he could do so much better.

"Well... here we go." Grabbing her keys of the table in the hall, she made sure all the lights were off and the windows locked before checking her hair one more time in the mirror by the door, then walking out.

Chapter Thirteen

Gavin

One lunch date, one kiss on the beach. That was it, but something about her stirred him. Sure, she looked like the girl from the beach. Hell, she *was* the girl, but she wasn't. The girl on the beach was timid, a frightened girl in a delicate shell. The girl he was waiting for—she was tough, like a hard candy, deliciously sugary outside, her insides something he hoped to find out more about tonight. His dream: that the hard shell encased a sweet, soft filling. It was like there were two sides to her. Since they had reconnected here in town, the tough attorney had been in control at all times, except for the small glimpses of the free spirit, the soft-hearted girl he had met on the beach and seen during their lunch date. He had a sneaking suspicion that the hardness was all an act. One he hoped to crack.

He had asked her over for dinner. Everything was

ready. The roast was so perfect it would melt in her mouth, and the lighting spoke of romance. Candles shone from every surface, the gentle flicker of the flames bouncing off the walls around them. He had prepared his bedroom on the off chance that she did stay, that they could take this chemistry to the next level, but he was not going to push that.

The sound of tires pulling up on the gravel that covered the circular drive at his home inside town was music to his ears as he strode across the dark wood floor toward the overly large front door. Pulling it wide, he smiled broadly as she came around her car. "Hello, beautiful."

"Hello yourself." She stood still, just watching him from mere steps away; he could tell she was deep in thought, the hard walls so high they were visible, but to him it was a sign begging him to scale it. Sure steps took him to her, and with a quick motion, he wrapped his arm around her waist and pulled her the rest of the way to him, capturing her lips with his. He could tell it caught her off guard by the way her body tensed, becoming rigid in his arms. The minute she relaxed, he deepened the kiss,

111

becoming firmer, his tongue gently pressed forward to taste her lips just a bit before pulling back and catching the heated look in her lidded eyes.

"Mmmmm, you taste heavenly." Releasing her lips and setting her back on the ground, he kept his arm around her waist as he led her inside. Walking behind her, he couldn't help watching her move; her legs covered in those jeans were long and lean. Her ass was held so perfectly in the tight material. It was going to take all he had to not skip the meal and entertainment and just take her to bed.

"Nice home." Caitlin smiled up at him before continuing her visual perusal.

He smiled, enjoying the way she seemed to be taking in everything.

"You decorate it yourself?"

He nodded as he led her toward the kitchen. "Yes, I didn't want that stuffy, uncomfortable look when I came home. I wanted to feel like I could just be me here."

Her smile filled him with hope. "You accomplished it. I feel comfortable already. Like I could just sit in the corner and read a book or something."

112

He pointed to the big gray overstuffed chair in the corner, surrounded on two sides by floor-to-ceiling bookshelves filled to the brim with leather-bound volumes from every great writer and a few new up-and-coming authors as well.

"Make yourself at home anytime then." Walking toward the table that sat in the middle of the room, he pulled out a chair. "Your seat, ma'am."

Chapter Fourteen

Caitlin

Sitting at the perfectly set table, each piece of flatware seemed meant for that very spot, as if he had precisely chosen each one. For some reason, it felt like a real home, something so perfectly cozy and welcoming, anyone who came in had no chance but to feel it. How a man that just put off an air of control and complete no-nonsense could create such a happy, carefree home, she had no clue. Her mind was still reeling over the two sides of him: the GQ and the home-loving family man, can cook type man, when he took the lid off the pot; steam rose to fill the room, billowing out in a cloud, and the smell of a rich sauce bombarded her nose.

"Wow, a man that can cook and decorate, are you sure you're real?" When he reached over, she held up her plate as he served her. "That looks great and the smell is divine," she said as she breathed in.

"Thanks. Well, dig in."

Taking her fork, she took a piece of the meat and potato and brought it to her mouth. The flavor invaded her senses, and Caitlin found herself moaning as the meat melted on her tongue. "This is great."

"Oh, music!" Caitlin laughed as he pushed back from the table and headed over to the player on the table behind the couch. A few clicks of his fingers and contemporary sounds filled the room.

"Great choice, is that Blue October?" Caitlin asked between bites.

"Yes it is. I have always liked them."

"Me too." She took a sip of the wine that perfectly paired with the roast.

"So, you're in advertising. Why?" Caitlin inquired.

"Well, really it came to me. I was helping my friend out to pay for college, working in the office and just doing what ever he asked. Eventually I just changed my major, worked for him for a while, then when his dad retired I

115

started on my own." Gavin sat back a bit from the table, setting down his napkin next to the plate on the table.

"Wow, impressive! I have always wanted my own firm; unfortunately, I just never worked up the guts to do it. However, you did all of that and now look at you. Seriously, I am impressed." Following suit, she pushed back from the table. "Thank you for dinner. It was amazing!"

"You, my dear, are welcome. Now for the entertainment." Gavin stood up, picking up the plates from the table. "Just let me put these in here."

"Here, let me help." Caitlin stood up, picked up the pot with the remaining roast and potatoes, and followed him through the archway. What she found as she crossed those arches would have made most professional chefs drool. Gavin's kitchen was a work of culinary art.

"Ok… You have been holding back. You said you could cook but you didn't tell me you had a world class kitchen in here."

Gavin chuckled as he grasped the tray she had just brought in, and quickly placed it in his subzero refrigerator. "Yeah, it's a hobby. I like the feeling I get when I create

116

something, and then watch my friends eat it and enjoy it. That is the best." Gavin waved his hand over the top of the faucet and water gently poured out. She watched him wash his hands before wiping them down with the rag that hung there to the side. Everything in this room perfectly matched, just like the other rooms she had seen.

"Well, that was quick work. And I must say you are much nicer company than the television I usually have on." She smiled as she noted the small flat screen sitting on the end of the counter.

Placing the dishrag she had used to dry her hands back on the hook, Caitlin smiled up at him. His eyes met hers and her breath hitched. Something about him just sent her body into a surge. Just the smallest look and her pulse raced as her body came alive. "I could not leave you to clean up after the meal you just made me. It was spectacular. I may have to hire you to cater my next event. I mean, you may be good at advertising, but you have a clear gift in the kitchen."

The sun had begun to set as they made their way out of the kitchen. He led her to the back wall of his home; she was amazed at the view through the glass overlooking the deck set over the Seattle skyline. With a quick movement, he flipped a latch, and slid the glass door into the wall. The sky was literally right in front of them and Caitlin took a few steps out onto the cedar deck.

"So beautiful. How do you ever leave this place? I would work from home." The pale pink hue of the sun settling between the tops of the evergreen trees that framed the lake in front of them created a living painting, mesmerizing her. Turning from the beauty in front of her, she snaked her arms up his chest to lock them around his neck. She just wanted give him a quick peck, just enough to say 'Hey, I like you, and oh yeah, thanks for the meal.' "Thank you for tonight. I really enjoyed it."

She did not want to leave, she wanted to stay; the two times they had been together, he had been nothing but respectful. Innocent touches and caresses that hadn't gone any further. Deep down, she wondered what it would be like, what his hands running along her skin, touching her, what his lips on her skin would feel like. The times he had touched her, even for those brief moments, he had done so with so much authority, desire, and need pulsing through him. His kisses had started a fire inside her, one she secretly hoped he would stoke until it consumed her completely. Was she willing to say it aloud, to put it out to him? Where the truth of her reality would infect it with the devastation of what would eventually happen, the betrayal, the hurt, the leaving, and in the end the broken hearts, the inevitability of her life.

"Then stay, Caitlin. Stay with me," Gavin said with a firmness that shocked her.

She felt his hand against her back, sliding beneath her shirt. The minute his strong fingers touched her bare skin, tingles of electricity flowed through her body, pulsing through every inch of her being. His body was in complete control of hers as he brought his head down, and like a magnet was pulling her to him, she lifted up to the tips of her toes and met his lips with hers. His lips claimed hers, plundering her mouth with his tongue, all the while walking her backward on his deck toward the sliding door that led to a different room than they had come from before. She did not care where they were going, as long as he continued kissing her. The heady mix of the flavor of his kisses with the smell of his cologne was gasoline to the fire already raging inside her. His body led her, his hands firm, his hips

119

against her. They slowly made their way to the other end of the deck, tongues dancing, and hands roaming.

As she walked backwards, completely engrossed by the feeling of his hands on her body, she felt the warmth of a fire that crackled in a fireplace along the far wall of whatever room they were entering. The second his lips left hers she took the chance to look around. Rich, dark colors accented the dancing flames, the large bed in the center of the room definitely the focal point. Nothing was out of place. Just like him and the rest of his house, it was perfect.

She pushed back from his chest. "You are so trying my resolve here, Gavin." For each step back she took, he took one closer; the determination and raw sexual desire showing in his eyes caused her pulse to race.

"I want you, Caitlin. I want to feel you under me, your soft skin under my fingers, taste you on my lips. I think you want that, too. I think you want to feel, to let go of that hard shell you have built up so far around you that the idea of anything more is just too much. I am the man to get through that shell, to break that wall. Let me, Caitlin. Give yourself to me."

She shook her head. The words he said rang so true

it was as if he were reading the words from her soul. If she let him in, then what? What would happen if he got tired of her? What if he thought that those dark desires that turned her on made her crazy, or worse yet, mentally unhealthy as she had heard so many times before? Before she could say anything, he moved across the room, seizing her in his arms, his lips once again claiming hers as his deft fingers found the edge of the spaghetti straps and slowly pushed them off her shoulders. His lips left hers and slowly kissed their way down her neck to that hollow spot that just sent her over the edge. Breathing quickly, Caitlin couldn't tell if she was going to just pass out. Each kiss sent sensations racing through her: pleasure and desire filling her very soul. Knees weakening, she gave just a bit, and before she lost her footing completely, he had his arm around her, holding her close. She felt his hard shaft against her stomach through the material of her clothes. Instantly, all questions disappeared. It had been too long, way too long.

Chapter Fifteen

Gavin

One minute they were kissing and he could feel the desire in her rising, and the next he felt that wall of hers shift into place. He pulled back just a bit, looking into her eyes. He wanted her; he needed her, yet he wanted her to give herself to him. This was something he knew deep down she would do. Today was not it. Dammit, he wanted it to be!

"Caitlin, I understand if you're not ready." He brushed a lock of hair out of her eyes, the soft tresses moved behind her ear easily, and he relished the feel. "I can wait. I will wait. Until you are." Brushing a light kiss on Caitlin's lips, tasting the flavor of her, before forcing his body to pull back from the warmth of hers, despite the fact that her hands had reattached themselves to his shirt, clenching and pulling him forward. "When you are ready, then there will be no hesitation, and that is when we will move forward. I just found you, Caitlin. I do not intend to let you go. So don't worry. This is not the end. Trust me on this."

Gavin took her hand in his and led her through the door from his bedroom, past the closed door to his other room, and then his office just beyond. When the hall opened up to the main room of the home where the night had started hours earlier he stopped, pulling her to him one more time. This time she came willingly. Yet, she had yet to say anything. Her mind was running miles a minute, he could tell she wanted to say something; what, he had no clue.

"Gavin, I am just not ready. I want to be so bad. I really do. You are everything I could want. But I'm just not. I thought I was ready; I wanted to be with you so badly. I really did. I just need to take it slow. I hope that is ok... I just, well ... is that ok?" Her heartfelt words, filled with fear, hit him deep.

"Of course it is. Look. We had a wonderful evening. Let's just call it a night and we can do this again if you want. Anytime." Gavin did his best to control the demand in his voice. He didn't want to scare her away.

123

Something about her screamed the need for acceptance. That was something he intended to give her.

Walking her out the door, down the steps to her car, the silence between them seemed to loom around them, despite the crunch of the gravel beneath their feet echoing through the dark night. Reaching out he opened the door to her small car, ushering her inside before closing the door carefully. The window slid down as he stepped back.

"I had a great time, Gavin. Thank you." Caitlin's voice shook just a bit; he knew she was holding back tears. The realization shook him to his core.

"Me too, Caitlin. Me too. I'll call you. Drive safe now." Waving as she backed down to the turnaround in the drive, Gavin watched as the red taillights drifted off into the night.

***

"Yes, Shelly." Gavin looked over the screen in front of him. The uncut version of the latest commercial was playing scene by scene as he took notes on what edits he wanted completed.

"You have a package, want me to bring it in?"

"I'd appreciate that. I mean, you *are* my assistant. Seems the appropriate thing to do." Gavin clicked the intercom release button and returned to the screen. Even the sound of his door opening and closing and Shelly's shuffling across the carpet was not enough to stop him. The past two days had gone by and every second seemed to be getting longer and longer. He was certain that he had lost his touch. Two women he truly had interest in; one would more than likely have started out sexually but the other, that had been done the standard, meet innocently way and wine and dine her first. Yet, she too had run away. He called her the next day, but received the cold shoulder from her assistant. Leaving a message was his only option and he took it. The problem was he never heard back. Part of him tried to reason that maybe her assistant had out of some sort of protective instinct erased his message. Nevertheless, the other part of his mind screamed at him that he had scared her away. That he was too much.

"Thanks, Shelly, I'll take it from here." He turned to the package and glanced up to see Shelly silently close the door behind her as she left. Carefully removing the brown paper wrap on the package, unsure of what was in the box, he found his curiosity peaked as he saw the periwinkle blue and white scrollwork.

"What the hell?'

Removing the remainder of the wrapping was a quick job; pulling the card off the top he opened the flap and stopped breathing as he read.

Gavin,

Thank you for the wonderful evening. I am so sorry for calling you back, but I needed to think about a few things. If you are willing, I would love to see you again. Maybe if you are interested you could accompany me to a gallery opening. I have included the invite and a little something as thanks. I hope to see you there.

Yours truly,

Caitlin

He tore open the box in seconds; laughter bellowed as he saw what was inside. The box contained a single container of super glue, with a little note to use it to glue her car door shut so she would not be able to run away.

He was going to that opening. Nothing would keep him from it or her.

126

Chapter Sixteen

Caitlin

Caitlin brushed the black dress down her body, making sure it lay just right. It had to be perfect; looking one more time in the mirror, she twirled just a bit like a little girl in a fancy dress. She felt beautiful.

"Sarah, well, what do you think?"

Sarah came in from the kitchen holding a can of seltzer and a large soft pretzel. "Holy hell. You look great! I knew you would. That dress looks made for you, I swear. Now go put on my shoes, I want to see the full look."

Making quick work of the slingback three-inch heels Caitlin stood tall and did a little catwalk for her best friend. "And the verdict is? Sarah?" Caitlin stopped and turned toward her friend. "Oh, Sarah! What's wrong?"

"Nothing is wrong! It's all right! You look

amazing. I mean it. Now get your butt going and remember what we talked about."

Wrapping her arms around her friend loosely, Caitlin smiled as she released her. "Thank you for your help with this. I mean you're right; I have to try. Not every guy out there is going to be out to hurt me. Not everyone can be my family; the world teems with happy couples and families. I just need to get my chance… Right. Now, I'm off. Have fun tonight, because I know I am." Caitlin waved as she made her way out the door home and down to ground level.

***

Caitlin walked through the exhibits, taking time at each one, all the while scanning the crowd for Gavin. When the trays went by again, carried by wait staff in the white shirts and black pants typical of catered events she grasped another glass of champagne. She had just finished taking a final swig from her third glass when she heard a cough behind her. Turning on the ball of her right foot, she stopped face-to-face with Gavin.

"You came!" She tried to hold back the smile that erupted on her face but it was hopeless. She had convinced
128

herself that he was going to come then after about twenty minutes of waiting, done the opposite. Talked herself through the sadness that she thought she was going to have to deal with. But—he had come!

"Yes I did, sorry I was late. I had to finish up with some work. You know clients, always thinking they are the only things you have to do. You look lovely, stunning really. I'm surprised I didn't have to fight off a crowd of men to get to you."

"You're fine, and definitely no crowds of men here, just artwork; well, I did see one of the waiters giving me the eye but I think that was because I took the last of the champagne he had... Again." She started walking towards the next exhibit, loving the feeling of his hand on her back, the way it guided her each time they moved. Their conversation was filled with comments on the different pieces, until they made it back to the one they had started at, and his hand had started to roam further than her back.

"Did you eat?" Gavin asked as they walked out into the Seattle night.

"Yes, earlier. I always try to before these things. The champagne, you know," she said trying to think of some way to extend the night.

"How about you come to my place for dessert?" His eyes filled with sultry desire. She had no doubt that if she went to his house where they would end up. The tension between them was so thick you could probably cut it with a knife.

"I would love that, except I took a cab." Before she could continue, he was turning towards the valet and handing him a slip of paper.

"That's no problem. I drove. I promise to bring you back as soon as you want to go home." Caitlin smiled and nodded at his comment.

"Good, now that we have that settled, I have something I have been dying to do all night." Gavin's sure voice was thick with desire. She knew what he was going to do and found herself leaning into him for the kiss. Their lips touched and the world around them fell away. Her hand slid up his chest, feeling the hard muscles beneath the material of his dress shirt. The valet's cough broke their fervent kisses.

"Thank you." Caitlin followed him around the car,

taking her place in the passenger side. When Gavin slid into his and shut the door, she felt her pulse race; his hand went right to her thigh, making little circles on her leg, and each movement sent her desire skyrocketing.

The drive to his home went quickly since the nightlife of Seattle left the roads clear for the most part, and when they pulled into his driveway, she was ready.

"Wait there."

She watched him come around the car to her door, opening it up and reaching his hand toward her. This was it, the moment that meant everything. Caitlin knew it and she was ready, which was what she kept telling herself. There were no awkward silences with him. He was so strong and yet so approachable. She lifted her hand into his, letting him pull her from the car, directly into his arms.

Each step toward the house was filled with kisses, and she had no idea how they made it, but they did. Once inside the house their hands roamed freely, she felt so desired, and her pulse beat so fast she felt she could pass out. His kisses took the breath from her, and just when she thought she could take no more he released her mouth just long enough to trail more down her neck.

131

"Oh, Gavin." Her fingers started working on his shirt as they made their way down the hall toward his room. When they made it through the door, he held a finger up to his mouth and she quickly closed her lips, biting them a bit as she watched him move around the room. One switch flipped and the fireplace came alive. Another and the lights turned off. Yet another caused the sconces on the wall to come alive, flickering like little flames. Then he hit one more and music filled the air. Caitlin watched him walk toward her, moving in rhythm to the music just a bit. The smile on his face was a sweet treat. His lips found her neck, placing little kisses there; Caitlin raised her hands a bit to reach for him.

"Nope. Not yet. My turn." She stopped, letting her arms fall to her sides as he explored her neck and collarbone area with his lips. When he reached the straps to her dress, she felt him slide them off her shoulder, the silky material sliding slowly down her body. Instantly she felt a bit self-conscious, knowing she wore no bra that evening, but his mouth claimed hers once more and she was again lost in him.

Chapter Seventeen

Gavin

Ecstasy. She was just that. Not one for flowery words unless working on an ad campaign, he thought of her as every flowery word combined into one. Gavin's tongue trailed a path down her neck as her dress slipped further down her body toward the floor. Her rounded breasts were now revealed to him, the tips pebbled with the desire. Breathing raggedly, his tongue lapped at her hardened nipple before moving onto the next, her hand grasping his head as if in encouragement. Encouragement was something he did not need. Hell, he wanted to claim her, own her, show her the deep, dark desires that he knew so well and had no doubt she would desire just as much. He wanted to protect her and keep her. The idea of sharing her repulsed him; she would never be a sub he could share at a club, he wanted every inch of her succulent body all to himself, splayed for his devouring, and he would devour her. Every

133

part of him craved her, pushing him toward her, begging him to take her, to own her. As he continued his exploration with his hands he guided the dress further, exposing her body to him. He suckled on her ample breasts while his hand slid downward and the dress fell the rest of the way to the floor.

She stood there in just the barest of lace panties, wet with her desire. She was stunning, everything he ever wanted... except for one thing. The one thing that mattered most to him for long-term co-existence—she was not a submissive. Hell, she did everything to not be submissive, which completely confused him, because her very essence screamed natural submissive. A woman who needed the one thing he could give her... him.

"You're beautiful," he said, his lips against her stomach, making her flinch. "Don't pull away, I mean it. You are stunning. Everything I have ever dreamed of in a woman."

"No, I'm not. But good line anyway."

He stood up, looked down into her eyes. "No. It's not a line; I mean it." With a swift movement, he picked her up, carried her across the room, and placed her on his bed.

He looked down at her prone form, desire now evident as her mouth opened just enough that he could see the tip of her tongue as it slipped out and licked her thick, pouty bottom lip. God, he wanted that tongue swirling around his cock, which with every movement of her tongue pulsed against his clothing and would surely leave a scar if it did not get released from its confines. With her eyes looking him up and down, he let his hand slide down to his rigid shaft, letting his hand graze the hardness through the material of his pants, as her eyes got bigger and followed his movements.

Reaching out, he clasped her ankle and moved it to the right, giving him unfettered access to her barely-covered sex. His eyes never leaving hers, he reached up to grasp the top of the lace separating him from what he thought of as his personal heaven. With a gentle but firm tug, the bit of sheer material slid down her legs as she lifted slightly from the bed, allowing him to proceed. If her gaze slipped from his, he knew she'd most likely backtrack and retreat to the corner of herself where she felt more comfortable. Her carefully constructed wall had obvious cracks in it, making him determined to push through them, hoping that on the other side was his fantasy.

Gavin's fingers slid up her legs, leading the way for his mouth as he kissed and nipped his way up her smooth skin. Reaching the apex of her thighs, he blew gently across her glistening sex. A smirk crossed his lips at her shiver and sigh before he let his tongue flick the exposed, hardened nub. Desire surged through him. He wanted to bury himself deep inside her, lose himself, and be the Master of her body, her mind. Lapping at her pussy, his swollen shaft ached to be where his tongue was currently pushing forward like a small cock, making circular movements, teasing then thrusting deep, tasting the flavor of her arousal.

Caitlin's cries, calling his name, were like permission to continue his ministrations with his tongue, but he didn't want to just stop there, and he paused his attention on her succulence and moved upward. His fingers replaced his tongue as his mouth trailed up her silky skin. Teasing her body with kisses and licks as he progressed, her shivers reward enough for the attention he was giving freely. When his tongue ringed around her hardened nipples, her back arched, and the moan that escaped her sweet mouth nearly undid him.

Releasing the turgid peak, he repeated the process

on the other side, and he was not disappointed when it brought the same heady reaction. His body needed to release, and he was sure as hell not going to deny it. Quickly, he stood, watching the look of need on her face. Despite the pain of the need to claim her, he took his time, controlling the situation even more than he already was. His hands worked the buttons separating the front of his shirt, her gaze heated as she watched. When he saw the tip of her tongue slide between those sexy lips, he almost ripped his clothes off. Sliding his belt off, the ping of the buckle reverberated through the air as it hit the floor. Slight as it was, her heightened breath was the only noticeable thing, but he noticed, saw, and felt everything; each movement of her body was blatantly obvious to him, so telling, just like it was a private language spoken only by him.

His only concern was Caitlin and what she needed. Part of him, deep down, questioned if she knew she was submissive, if something inside her craved what he could give, or even knew what that was. The questions raced through his mind; did he test her and see how she responded? Run the risk of losing her, when she was so much of what he needed, even if it was missing that one oh-so-important part? His pants hit the floor, pooling at his

137

feet, before he leaned forward, bracing himself on the bed. Watching her eyes filled with a look of complete wanton desire, he walked over to the side of the bed, his heavy cock bobbing as he walked, her gaze not wavering, only her tongue slipped out just a bit before she quickly slipped it back in and bit her bottom lip. Knowing it would tease her higher he grasped his aching member, letting his hand slide up and down as he reached into the drawer of the nightstand and pulled out the little foil pouch. Making his way to the end of the bed, he tore open the pouch and made sure his movements were nice and steady as he sheathed his cock. Only then did he turn his attention fully onto her, and there was no way that was going to change. As he moved forward, he captured her lips with his and grasped his cock, positioning it just at the entrance of her wet, silky entrance. Barely breaching her heat, his teeth clenched as the fire called to him. He wanted her, wanted his cock surrounded by her heat. Eyes shrouded in desire, her lips stopped moving as if caught in some trance, her mouth changing to an "O" as he slowly slid inside her. Each inch stretched her walls, and it took every ounce of his willpower to go slowly despite the quivering walls of her sex pulling and milking his cock. Fully seated, he looked into her eyes, and the word he heard was music to his ears.

"Please."

That was it.

He started to move; his hips thrust forward, his cock buried deep inside her, before pulling and retreating backward. With each pull from her body, his cock felt like it was being held in place and urged back. Her sex cinched down on him, until he had no choice but to delve back into her molten heat again. The feeling was exquisite. Each powerful movement brought him close to the edge until her body shuddered around his cock and her cry of ecstasy rang through him. He pushed further and harder until he felt his own release surge from his body.

He lay there watching her as she slept. Her chest raised ever so gently, her body so still. She was his. He had no doubt. He'd spent years with others, and not once felt like he did now. It was as if fate had given him his other half. The thought of her in his life more than temporarily not only didn't repulse him, it made his heart beat faster as peace settled over him. His eyes rested on the space on her neck that had the smallest of indents. The place where his collar should reside, the visible sign she was his. For once,

139

that thought truly belonged to him. It wasn't some idea that had been placed or pushed on him, but something he wanted—no, craved—to do. Pulling her close to him, he closed his eyes, relishing the scent of her hair lying against him.

Chapter Eighteen

Caitlin

She woke in the middle of the night, her head on his chest, the steady beat of his heart something she had to fight against as it comforted and lulled her into a world where dreams existed and happiness thrived. His heavy arms wrapped around her protectively. The darkness around them, she hoped, hid the thoughts she felt surely showed all over her face. She was content, happy, satisfied. Hell, he was so good in bed. After their initial time, they had come together during the night repeatedly, sleeping just enough in between to replace their energy until finally they were both completely sated.

Nevertheless, was it everything she had secretly hoped? No. She could tell he was holding back. What, she didn't know, but obviously he was not ready to show that part of him to her yet. Slowly slipping from his embrace, she paused each time she felt him stir. As she stood up from the bed, she turned and looked at the man that had just given her tremendous amounts of pleasure. His body lay there exposed to her greedy eyes. His strong back led to the most exquisite ass—rounded and firm, she was sure he worked out on a daily basis. No way could someone just naturally have an ass like that. She was still amazed he was interested in her. She was not some model type—svelte and lithe. Noticing her bag on the table by the door she quickly grabbed it; making her way to a room off the bedroom she assumed to be the bathroom. *Well done.*

The room was decorated in a manly way, dark wood highlighting the white alabaster sinks and tubs, no big flowery displays, just some well-picked art pieces; it was perfect, not overbearing, not completely without comfort or that touch that said someone lived here.

He must have hired a decorator.

She quickly put her clothes on and pulled her brush out of her purse. Running the brush through her curls, she did her best to be quiet, but the sex had created a bit of a knot in her hair and when she pulled a bit, her brush flew from her hand and hit the bottom handle of the drawer on

142

the bottom of the cabinet. She padded to the bathroom door and gently pushed it open just a crack. He had rolled over but had not awoken. She carefully let the bathroom door close, holding it so that the only sound was the gentle whoosh of it fitting into the jamb. Turning back toward the mirrored cabinet area, she headed to pick up the brush, throwing it in her bag. Looking in the mirror, she quickly pinched her cheeks, hoping she didn't look like she had just had sex. Pulling her phone from her bag she quickly made a call to the local cab company; luckily for her they were able to have a car there in the matter of a few minutes. Thanking them quietly she hung up and looked in the mirror one more time.

Who am I kidding; I did just have sex. Oh well. Better to leave now than in the morning with no time to change for work.

Stealing out of the bathroom, she quietly padded across the room toward the door, turned the handle gently and every time a noise clicked or clinked, she would check on Gavin. With no movement from him, she made her way out and down the hall.

I can't just go. I have to leave a note, at least.

143

Coming to a door on the left, she pushed it open and found a pitch-black room. Feeling along the wall to the right where most light switches were, she pressed the switch upward. The bright light filled the room, exposing an office that said luxury. A rich cherry desk was front and center on the plush tan rug. When she stepped in, it was as if the carpet came up to meet her. One wall filled with books as well as sporadic knick-knacks. She wanted to take the time to look at each and every thing that he displayed, knowing that it would tell her something about him—maybe the part of him he didn't show. But she knew that he would wake eventually, and then she would have to answer the question of why she was running. Again. She made her way around the desk and looked around for a pen. Nothing was out of place on his desk. His files were perfectly stacked. There were no receipts lying around, notes on stickies, no anything.

Damn, he is organized!

She opened the middle drawer, thinking that there might be a pen in there. Sure enough there was and she smiled as she reached for it. She looked around for paper but found nothing—just rulers, color wheels, and other

144

design things. Sitting down in his chair, she pulled open the top drawer on the right and spotted a pad of paper. She started a note just to let him know why she left; giving him the reason, she was willing to admit, at least. When she penned the final big spiral of her signature, she set the pen where she found it and pushed the drawer shut. About to stand up and head out, the spotlight on the bookcase on the other side of the room caught her attention. Her breath caught in her throat.

No way, not even possible.

Shock ran through her system as she walked closer to that highlighted item. With each step, she saw more of the detail—the lines that identified this creation as a one-of-a-kind piece. Standing directly in front of it, she had no doubt it was the same one. The man that she had been getting to know was, in fact, her mystery date. Trying to control the panic as her chest tightened and her breath started to catch in her throat, she quickly turned and ran from the room, no longer caring if she made noise. She had to get out. The front door to his home did nothing to slow her down as she tore out of the house and down to her waiting cab. The purr of the engine was the sound of her freedom coming to her, ready to take her away.

Don't do it. Just don't look.

But Caitlin did, and in that instant, she saw him standing on his porch, his bare chest exposed, his legs covered in lounge pants, a look of complete confusion on his face as he watched her go. She turned her eyes forward, wiping away the tear that had fallen onto her cheek.

Chapter Nineteen

Gavin

"You mean to tell me she literally dropped off the face of the earth? Leaves you a note and boom… nothing? One day after a night with you?" Gavin looked up at Matt, who stood holding two cold bottles of beer. As he took one for himself, he shook his head.

"Yeah, that's basically the truth, I guess. I have tried her office. They say she is out of the office for an extended time due to a family emergency. Her cases have been transferred to a different attorney. I just don't know what to think," he said with a shrug.

The beer quenched his thirst for fluids, but his thirst for Caitlin had done nothing but grow. Eight hours and 22 days had gone by, each one more frustrating than the one before. Driving by her home had done nothing—the lights stayed off, and the only person he saw going in and out was her assistant. Just days earlier, he'd noticed her assistant watching him and tore off on his bike, not wanting to look like a stalker or something. But as days passed, then turned into weeks, he just nodded at her before slowly pulling off. Each call to her office had become more personal, with their apologies that they could not help him, though they really wanted to.

"Sorry Gavin, she's not here. No, there has been no change. I will give her the message when she checks in, but I don't expect her to anytime soon."

He truly felt like her assistant wanted to tell him something to help him but was torn and couldn't. The excuses just kept coming; each had a common theme, and none of them did anything for him. She didn't know, was all the assistant would say, and his frustration would grow and grow.

"I only have one other idea where she might have run to. If I go after her, then I *will* look like a stalker." He set the beer down and picked up his pool cue; analyzing all the shot options he had, he bent over, pulled back the cue, and let it slide forward. The crack of the ball hitting the side of the table sounded like the starting bell at a horse race.

148

"Why would she run? I didn't get all Dom on her. I actually behaved, if you can believe it. Completely vanilla." The smirk on Matt's face was priceless.

"You ever think that maybe, just maybe, that was what she wanted? Maybe she thought you were dull?" Laughter filled the room as Matt looked at the pool table.

"I do worry about that. Really, how do I fix it if that's the problem? If she avoids me like this, I won't even have a chance to show her." His head lifted at the clink of stilettos on the stone floor.

"Hey, Sonja."

"Hello, stud. Girl problems?" Gavin watched the woman walk to her husband, the smile on his friend's face mirrored by the glow of sheer love on Matt's wife's.

"Yeah. Of course, it's not like you have a twin out there." He winked at Sonja as she sat on her husband's lap.

"Well, have you tried to just tell her how you feel?" Sonja asked, looking truly concerned.

Gavin shook his head. "I would if I could, but I can't find her."

"You can't find her? Not at all? Seriously? After the way you met, and the dates you two went on, and you a) didn't tell her how you felt, and b) don't know where she goes to think?"

He did know where Caitlin would go to think. Had all along. He would have to do this right or he would look like a crazy stalker. "Look, I have to go... You're both right. I do know where she probably is. It's time. Time to collect what's mine."

Chapter Twenty

Caitlin

"I'm not running and definitely not hiding." Caitlin looked at the face on her computer. Video chat had become the newest ritual in her life. Vivian would call daily, begging her to come back to the office—to her life.

"He was not at your house today. I think it's safe. You scared off another one with your weird ways. Really…he was very attractive, and he treated you well. Hell, I was a bit jealous. I don't get it. Why did you leave?"

Picking up her mug of hot chocolate, Caitlin sipped slowly, the creamy marshmallows sweetening the chocolaty concoction. "He was not who he said or acted like. It was a game."

"Are you sure? Or was this like the last date you threw away because he had a thing for twirling your hair?"

She shook her head. "Nope. I am sure."

The knock on her beachside door caught her off guard. Setting down her cup, she looked at Vivian. "Hey, let me buzz you later okay? Someone is here. Probably one of my neighbors telling me that the shutters need to be up for the storm that's coming. Love ya." She hit the end button and pushed back from the desk. Her Capri-length sweatpants and oversized sweatshirt not necessarily what she wanted people to see her in right now, she shrugged. *Oh well.* It wasn't like she had someone to impress, and really in all likelihood, there never would be. Grabbing the scarf off the cabinet, she tied her hair up into a loose ponytail as she walked, the mass of unruly curls at least held back a bit from view.

Grasping the door handle, she pulled it open and stopped short. The breath in her chest expelled, and then she just held it. Seconds seemed like minutes before anything was said. She stood there looking at him in his rolled-up jeans and the white dress shirt, turned up at the sleeves and un-tucked, open low enough to show his spectacular, chiseled chest.

"Hello, Caitlin."

"Gavin, what are you doing here?" She turned and walked into her home, hearing his footsteps behind her.

Knowing now who he was... well... that turned everything around and upside down. She now understood the connection they had. He *was* everything in one package. However, he had not been dominant with her at all. Hell, he had not even been the one she thought he had been at the restaurant. Never after the lunch or dinner at his house or even after sex or during had he shown a bit of dominance. Then it hit her. The thing that he held back: he was everything she wanted and that scared the hell out of her. She kept thinking if he possibly was both of the people she had met, then there would be nothing to run from anymore. Except that she was so scared. Scared to find that out for herself if it was true and he was the perfect mix, the thought she possibly had that, well it scared the living shit out of her. There was nothing to stop her. Her dream of the perfect man stood there. Hell, give the man a white horse and he could carry her into the sunset.

"I came for you. I need answers."

She stopped in her tracks and gave him a hard look. "Answers, huh?"

Quickly, she went to the hutch that stood beside the door, opened the drawer, and pulled out her mask. Turning, she tossed it to him and watched as his face went completely white when it landed in his hand. He looked down, and she waited while he stood there quietly for what seemed like the longest time.

When he looked back at her, the look on his face changed and heat seared her from the look in his eyes. "It was you?" His voice came out deep and the vibration in it caused her pulse to beat faster.

"Yes, it was me. And you were my date?"

"How did you know? I never gave you any way of knowing." Gavin's head shook as he looked down at the mask, almost as if in shock.

Looking into his eyes, she took a deep breath. "I saw your mask in your office when I wrote that note." She shook her head. "If I only had tried the room to the right instead of the left. Maybe this would have been different."

"Stop." Gavin moved quickly, coming to stand right in front of her. Left with no other choice, she stood and let him tip her face up to his. "It would have ended the same.

The room to the left is my personal playroom. You would have figured it out."

Confusion. She was filled with confusion. The man she had started dating seemed so normal, not like a Dom. Nothing about him had seemed like the Doms she read about in books.

"I don't understand. I never saw you like that." Caitlin's voice came out almost in a whisper. The skin on her arms tingled as his fingers lightly slid up her arm.

"Why don't we walk on the beach while we talk?" She nodded silently as he guided her with his hand on her back.

They walked for a ways without saying anything. The seagulls cried and dove toward the gray water. The waves crashed, the storm stirring the waves.

"Caitlin, I fell for you the first time I saw you on this beach, with your windswept hair and the tangle of your sweatshirt. I had already signed on to that service. In answer to your comment, just because I was not constantly telling you what to do or how to do it does not mean anything. It just means I respect you. I want a woman that speaks her mind, who has a brain in her head. If I wanted a mindless puppet, I could have had that years ago. Submission is not about that. What do you know of being a submissive?"

She bit her lip and took a deep breath. "Well, from what I have read, romance novels, those groups on Facebook, you know, the girl kneeling. I had the kinky desires, the fantasies that won't quit. Hell, I even begged for it from some of my exes who basically said that what I was asking was a serious no, just abuse. The thing is, I get off on thinking about being tied up. The thought of someone taking a flogger to me makes me so hot I can't stand it. I want that. I just don't know how to get it." She sighed, ragged breath slipping through her lips as her shoulders relaxed and sadness took over her face. "But please don't think what we had was bad. It wasn't, it was great, but I need something more. That night at the restaurant, it was as if you were looking into my soul. I couldn't handle it. I wouldn't have been able to tell you no. Then when I saw that mask after I got to know you, it was as if my worlds collided; it was no longer going to be the world that I kept here at the beach and the world that was there in the city." Caitlin took a deep breath before continuing. "What if you were the one that I always dreamed about? You had my heart already. It was as if my fantasies were there… within reach… and, well, it scared me. You know my past; we talked about it. I find perfection, and then… it leaves…. I just figured I would cut to the chase and head it off."

When his hand closed on her upper arm, she stopped and turned toward him. The look on his face was enough to say "shut up," but when his finger came to her lips, she knew for sure. Just as he opened his mouth, thunder cracked and lightning flashed across the sky. In mere seconds, everything around them was pelted with rain; water surged and crashed around them, creating white foam as it churned. Bits floated into the air, looking like snow falling to the ground.

Gavin looked at her. "Enough. First, I'm not leaving. Second, our worlds were meant to collide, I truly believe that. Before you say it, no, I'm not selling you some line. Now, let's head back to your house before this storm gets out of control. I think it's about time you learned a bit more about what submission really is and what it's not."

Chapter Twenty-One

Gavin

Rain pummeled against his head as he held tightly to her hand as they ran toward her beach house. The storm was now in full effect: waves thrashed the beach and rain came down in sheets as the wind pushed it directly into them. When it seemed to get even harder, he stepped in front of Caitlin, his arm bent behind him, trying to keep her from getting hit by rain that felt like small knives hitting his skin. Finally, he saw the path to her home through the sand dunes; pulling her closer beside him they made their way to the small house. When he had her safely at the door, he grabbed her keys out of her shaking fingers, placed a small kiss on her lips, then turned and opened the door, holding it open with one arm as he led her through the opening, his other hand on her back.

"Thank you," Caitlin said, wiping the wetness from

her face, doing her best to hold in shivers from the cold rain and to hide herself from him. The rain had turned her clothes into form-fitting sweats, leaving nothing to the imagination. The material clung to her every curve. Finding it hard to concentrate on anything other than her body, he stood there watching her.

"You're welcome. Now, shall we get you out of these wet clothes?" Gavin's voice came out deeper, huskier, full of want. His large steps made quick work of the distance between them; his fingers clasped the bottom of her shirt, catching the look of excitement in her eyes and the way she bit her lower lip.

"What do you *really* know of the lifestyle?" Gavin asked, his voice demanding, yet kind; she felt compelled to answer.

She held her arms up as he pulled the shirt over her head. Inch by inch, he marveled at the silken skin that became exposed. Her firm breasts encased in the sexy lace cups of her bra only enticed him further. Trying to control the desire to take a hardened nipple into his mouth and warm it, he knew that she needed to understand that he was not going to control her the way she was so scared to find.

She would be vulnerable, and that made him want to cherish her, she was so naturally submissive. Ironically, if they had not signed onto that matchmaking site, they would have met anyway. Her timid voice brought him back.

"Honestly, just what I have read in books. And even that, well… it's not much. I just… well… I wanted something I haven't had before. Not that I have had it bad. Hell, you and I have talked about our past relationships."

He just nodded as she talked, he could tell she was trying to distance herself from the reality that he was now untying the drawstring on the pants she wore.

"I just wanted someone who could love me, someone who was not going to hurt me, not let me run anymore, hell, not make me. Well, I wanted that all-consuming kind of love that is in the books, the passion, the devotion of the Doms. They truly cherish their submissive. I want that. I want the passion in bed, I want the whole thing."

Her pleading eyes looked up at him, and he let go of the edge of her sweats, letting them slide down her legs to puddle at the floor. Reaching over to the chair draped with a soft blanket, he grasped the blanket and wrapped it around
160

her before pulling her to him.

"This is not just about rough sex and whips and handcuffs. It is about complete devotion. I do not want a puppet, someone who is just going to do what I say and not have a brain in her head. That is just, well…cheap. I want someone who, when we are in front of the fireplace, can talk about the day they had. Do I want that someone to be a submissive in my bed? Yes, most definitely yes. I want that more than anything, but I won't force it on you. I love you, Caitlin. I have always loved you. I just didn't know it was you. I was drawn to the girl I met on the beach and in Seattle, but I craved the girl I met through the dating service. But guess what? Alone, neither girl would have been enough. I need both. I need that submissive girl, the one who is willing to learn… the one I see before me. The natural submissive, and the strong independent attorney."

"I don't know how to be submissive, Gavin."

He shook his head. "Not true. Yes, you do. And what you don't know, I will teach you. But you, my dear, are submissive." Reaching up, he wiped the tear that had fallen from her eye. "Now, do you want to learn? Or are you going to run again? Because I want you in my life for a long

161

time, and I am willing to prove that to you. Plus, I know where you run to. Unless you have another beach house I don't know about."

The smile on his face couldn't have been removed for any reason when she nodded her head yes. When she let the blanket fall away, exposing her to him once again, his world felt complete. Gavin knew he had found the one for him, and he was going to spend the rest of his life proving it to her. Holding out his hand, he helped her up, all the while taking a quick glance around, noting the open doorway and the bed beyond. "Yours?" He nodded towards the open door.

"Yes." Her voice a whisper of approval. With a smile, he proceeded to lead her that way.

Chapter Twenty-Two

Caitlin

Caitlin followed him to her bedroom and with remarkable ease; Gavin took control of her world. When he turned toward her, his face burned with desire that she was sure was mirrored in her own. His fingers brushed over both her shoulders, taking the bra straps with them. With her bra now just holding on by the back strap, Caitlin waited, barely breathing, for him to do whatever he wanted. And the funny thing was, she wasn't worried or scared. She knew it would be okay. His head lowered and she felt his hot breath against her skin as his tongue reached beneath the edge of the lace that barely covered her nipple. When she felt the brush of his tongue against her, she couldn't help but moan in response, her body coming alive. If it weren't for his grasp holding her upright, she would have fallen to the floor completely overwhelmed.

"Please, Gavin!" Caitlin cried; when his tongue caused little shots of pleasure to pulse through her body, she threw her head back.

"Please what, Caitlin? Say the words."

Caitlin was so caught up in his touch that when his hand drifted to the edge of her lace panties, she almost died right there. But she didn't and his hand didn't stop, it made its way further down, staying on the outside of her lace covering, tempting and teasing her sex with his masterful fingers.

"Take me! Please! Take Me!" she screamed out as he toyed with her, rubbing the lace against her sensitive skin.

"Not good enough. Tell me exactly what you want. I want to hear you say the words." Gavin's voice came out so raspy, full of desire.

She was not prepared for this. She had assumed it was going to be just like last time. Great sex, but just that… sex. This was more—way more.

"Where do you want my finger to go? Let's start that way," Gavin instructed, voice firm.

164

She bit her lip; she knew what she wanted. Did she dare? Finally, the teasing became too much as his fingers and mouth worked their magic on her body.

"Please, on my skin. I want your fingers on my skin." His fingers traced the edge of her panties and pulled them to the side. The first touch of his fingertip on the lips of her heated sex was enough to send her into a small orgasm. As it rolled through her, she couldn't help it. She needed more. "More. Please…more."

Gavin eased a finger into her hot, wet core and then as she became used to it, she felt him add a second before starting to move them in and out. Fucking her with just his fingers, his thumb brushed over her clit, the circular motion matching the speed of his fingers thrusting deep inside. Then suddenly, they were gone and he was standing there in front of her as he pulled his shirt over his head and tossed it to her dresser. Biting her lip from the lack of touch, which left her empty and wanting, she looked at the sculpted god before her. His chest was chiseled in a way that she had only dreamed about. She could tell he really wanted her, not only for the night and not only on his arms at functions, but he really wanted her. The way he looked at her with so much desire, like he could eat her up.

"Come here, Caitlin," Gavin growled.

She just nodded and did as requested, despite the nervous tension inside of her; his look of complete adoration gave her confidence. Her heart felt as if it were beating out of her chest, but she wanted him in a way that she didn't know she could feel. When she was right in front of him, he placed his hand on her shoulder and she felt the gentle push and instantly knew what he wanted. Caitlin lowered herself to her knees and started to reach up to the bulge that was begging to be released from his pants.

"No. You will just kneel and do as I direct." He undid his slacks and pulled out his hardened cock. A clear drop of his desire pearled on the tip, and she did everything she could to stay still, desperately wanting to taste him.

"Open your mouth, Caitlin." Doing as he directed, he placed the head of his thick cock on her tongue, and she couldn't help but moan when his taste filled her mouth. With his hand at the back of her head, he started thrusting into her mouth. Her tongue wrapped around the head of his cock each time it came to rest on the edge of her lips. She could feel every ridge of him, thick and hard, as he thrust

166

back in, sliding along her tongue and easing his way down her throat. Quicker and quicker he moved, until she felt the pulsing in his cock as it grew even thicker and longer and spurted his essence down her throat. She swallowed with each pulse until he slowly pulled out and as he was about to pull completely away, she looked up at him with her eyes and met his. The joy in his gaze was evident; for once in her life, she felt like she had done well. She had made him happy.

Chapter Twenty Three

Gavin

Gavin had to control himself. Throwing her on the bed and taking her roughly was not going to teach her anything. Yes, she would enjoy it. He had no doubt of that. But tonight was going to be a mix of both worlds. Hard, demanding sex, and soft and gentle lovemaking. He lifted her face up to his with his finger under her chin and she readily followed his desires, standing with no questions.

"You will be mine. Only mine. You will do whatever I ask in this room or any other room of the house. Do you understand? I may not have my playroom here, but tonight you will be mine, to do with as I please. Do you understand?" He was so pleased when he saw her nod, he could have shouted to the world.

He pulled her to him and instantly his mouth claimed hers, their tongues dancing around each other as he

168

plundered her mouth, savoring her flavor. Laying her down on the bed, he saw the questioning look in her eyes as he walked toward her dresser and pulled a few of the scarves that were resting on the top off and brought them back to the bed. Clasping her right wrist, he affixed a scarf around it, tying it snugly and testing the tightness to make sure it wouldn't hurt her before repeating the process with the other end to a rung on her headboard. It was not the custom-made equipment he had at home, but this would work. He repeated the process on the other side before moving to her ankles and doing the same. Her eyes widened with each scarf, and when she found herself completely bared to him—wide open—his eyes roamed over her as she shuddered.

He slowly made his way from her ankle up toward her core, each kiss followed by a breath across the wetness left behind until he reached his goal. Her sex glistened, and her desire pooled on the bed beneath her as he licked from the base of her slit to the top of her clit, circling and probing with his tongue before flicking it and causing a scream of pleasure to escape her lips. When he rose up above her, he saw the blush that colored her cheeks, the smoldering desire evident in her eyes.

Grasping his cock, he positioned it at her entrance and pushed slowly inside, holding it at the edge as he reached up and tweaked a nipple. With each tug on it, he saw her breath catch, want causing her to rise up, forcing his cock in a bit further before he could pull back and repeat the process on the other side. The result was the same and before he knew it, he was deep inside her, his cock gripped by the walls of her tight core. Pulling back, he thrust again. Over and over he plunged inside her, her body at his complete disposal. His hands running everywhere, he felt her from top to bottom, learning every curve until he could take no more. He quickened the pace of his thrusts and when he felt her body cinch up on the edge of orgasm, he looked into her eyes and said two words, "Come, Caitlin." She shuddered around him, and he let his own release go. Able to breathe again, he released her ties and cuddled her to him. When he felt sleep overtake her, he relaxed, comforted that she had given herself to him. And that was just the start.

Epilogue

Caitlin stood on the beach the sun shining on her as she felt a pair of hands come around her. Instinctively, she leaned back against Gavin. They had been married now for six months, and it seemed like just yesterday, not two years ago, that they had met. Now they were not only married, she had been officially claimed. Collared. Wanted. She would never again run, and the man that held her now was the one she had dreamed about for years. She thought back to that morning when he had put the choker around her neck. Every guest had arrived just as Gavin and she had once, with the masks like theirs from that initial date; it was a perfect day, perfectly planned. The guest of honor, the woman that had matched them years before, helped them make sure that they were able to get enough masks custom made just for the day. The pièce de résistance had been the choker Gavin had given her: the garnet shone perfectly in the intricate, white gold encasement that held it around her neck. No one would know, or understand, the meaning of the stone. It was the color of his heart, so she could never doubt that he was always there, always his concern. She had tried to run a few times, but each time he chased her down. Now, she would never run. She was home. Home in the arms of the Master of her heart.

***

Annabelle stood at the back of the ceremony watching the latest couple from her service to wed. She was so happy for Gavin and Caitlin. People deserved to be happy. When the glass of champagne was placed in front of her on the tall table, she smiled. "Thank you."

"You're welcome. You know, you should be up there getting married. You deserve it."

She smiled at her chauffeur, the man who handled everything for her dates, the driver who drove every girl, a man she trusted. "You know I'm not meant for that. God only gives someone so many chances at love. And when you've blown them all... well... It's gone. Plus, now I get to make sure everyone else is happy. I don't have to worry about it anymore." She took a sip of the champagne and stood up. "Okay. I'm ready to go. You?" She headed toward the car, oblivious to the look of desire on the face of the
172

man she'd just walked away from.

Acknowledgments

I have so many people that have put up with my imagination and through it all had faith and patience while I figured out that those glimpses of imagination were really stories just waiting to be told.

Brett for putting up with my hours on the laptop, lack of attention, and one word answers. I still remember the first time he read my first chapter and said. You really can write. You made me laugh then and you do still today.

Kim, your faith and unwavering friendship is an inspiration. You have shown me that giving up is not the option, and for that I will always be grateful. Your belief in my writing and my stories has held me firm on the path to this book. Thank you for you. You are my person.

To the girls at A.P.I. your friendship, support, hours reading my chapters and putting up with my insecurities have shown me that family is not always who you are born into but who you meet along the way. You are my family of support and love. Love you all.

Grace, who despite everything still shows me that friendship, is not conditional but unconditional. You are the truest heart I know. Thank you for you. I can never repay your faith.

Lastly but not least, my children who inspire me daily, pushing me to reach my goals, and strive to show that anyone can achieve their dreams.